Minna C. Smith

The World and its People

Book III - our own country

Minna C. Smith

The World and its People
Book III - our own country

ISBN/EAN: 9783337227173

Printed in Europe, USA, Canada, Australia, Japan

Cover: Foto ©Andreas Hilbeck / pixelio.de

More available books at **www.hansebooks.com**

THE

WORLD AND ITS PEOPLE.

Book III.

OUR OWN COUNTRY.

BY

MINNA C. SMITH.

EDITED BY

LARKIN DUNTON, LL.D.,

HEAD MASTER OF THE BOSTON NORMAL SCHOOL.

SILVER, BURDETT & CO., PUBLISHERS,

NEW YORK ... BOSTON ... CHICAGO.

1894

PUBLISHERS' ANNOUNCEMENT.

——◆◆◆——

IT is now conceded by all educators that school instruction should be supplemented by reading-matter suitable for use by the pupil both in the school and in the home. Whoever looks for such reading, however, must be struck at first with the abundance of what is offered to schools and parents, and then with its lack of systematic arrangement, and its consequent ill adaptation to the needs of young people.

It is for the purpose of supplying this defect, that the publishers have decided to issue a series of volumes, under the general title of the YOUNG FOLKS' LIBRARY FOR SCHOOL AND HOME.

These books are intended to meet the needs of all children and youth of school age; from those who have just mastered their first primer, to those who are about to finish the high-school course. Some of the volumes will supplement the ordinary school readers, as a means of teaching reading; some will re-enforce the instruction in geography, history, biography, and natural science;

while others will be specially designed to cultivate a taste for good literature. All will serve to develop power in the use of the mother-tongue.

The matter for the various volumes will be so carefully selected and so judiciously graded, that the various volumes will be adapted to the needs and capacities of all for whom they are designed; while their literary merit, it is hoped, will be sufficient to make them deserve a place upon the shelves of any well-selected collection of juvenile works.

Each volume of the YOUNG FOLKS' LIBRARY will be prepared by some one of our ablest writers for young people, and all will be carefully edited by Larkin Dunton, LL.D., Head Master of the Boston Normal School.

The publishers intend to make this LIBRARY at once attractive and instructive; they therefore commend these volumes, with confidence, to teachers, parents, and all others who are charged with the duty of directing the education of the young.

SILVER, BURDETT & CO.

PREFACE.

THIS volume is designed to supplement regular instruction in the geography of the United States. It is not intended to take the place of the teacher, but to strengthen the impression which the teacher has made.

All formal instruction in geography should be preceded by systematic and well-directed observation of the phenomena of the earth and of the heavens as these phenomena are manifested in the neighborhood in which the children live. The study of the home should be so thorough that the children will have all the elementary ideas which they need in forming adequate conceptions of those portions of the earth and the heavens which lie beyond the range of direct perception.

During this process of immediate observation, all the ideas gained should be so connected with plans and maps that the children will be able, through the use of maps, to construct accurately, in their imaginations, the real world as it actually exists.

When this preparation of the children has been made, regular instruction in geography may be begun. Now maps are very helpful, especially in the hands of competent teachers. But the pupils should be led beyond the map, and be helped to create in the imagination what the map represents. With this creation should be connected the words which name the parts of the world and their relations to one another.

After this teaching has extended to those portions of the United States which are covered by this book, the book itself may properly be put into the hands of the pupils, to be read by them either at home or in the class at school. By this reading, the pupils will be conducted through a review of what they have already learned, and at the same time their use of language will be improved.

It is recommended to teachers and parents that a good map of the United States be kept constantly before the children while reading this book, and that they be required to trace out on the map every place and journey mentioned. It is believed that if the book is used in this way, it will be useful to the pupil and helpful to the teacher.

LARKIN DUNTON.

BOSTON, June 30, 1890.

CONTENTS.

CONTENTS.

THE CAPITOL AT WASHINGTON

OUR OWN COUNTRY.

CHAPTER I.

IN WASHINGTON.

1. Our country is a very large one, as the boys and girls who read this book already know; but it is not easy to realize how large the country is. If you were in San Francisco, and wished to travel across the United States to Washington, you would be obliged to ride for six days and six nights in the cars.

2. A mile, you know, is not a very short distance to walk; yet if a person could walk twenty miles a day, it would take about five months to walk from one coast of our country to the other.

3. There are over sixty million people in the United States, yet there are many regions where one might travel for hundreds of miles and not see a house.

4. Wherever we live in this country of ours, we hear a great deal about the President, whose home is the White House at Washington. Men are elected in all of the states to go to Washington and serve in the government of which the President is the chief officer.

5. Washington is the capital, or head city, and in it is a great building called the Capitol, where the men meet who are elected to the government.

6. In looking at the picture of the Capitol, you see the broad, handsome steps leading up to the entrance. Imagine that you have walked up those steps. In the main entrance of the Capitol is a huge door of solid bronze. On its nine tall panels are pictures of scenes in the story of our country. You are certain to stop and look at these pictures before going on into the rotunda, as the great entrance hall is called.

7. A small church might easily stand in this hall, and there would be room for its spire to reach to a great height. All about you on the walls are paintings.

8. You could spend many pleasant days in

the Capitol, looking at the paintings and statues But now you will go on and look in at the men who have been elected to Congress from different parts of the country. They are in two long and wide halls, the Senate Chamber and the Hall of Representatives.

9. There are hundreds of men in these rooms, sitting about at desks, standing up to make speeches, writing, talking, sometimes laughing, and all busy about the affairs of the government.

10. The Vice-President of the United States is at the head of the Senate. The officer who presides in the other hall is known as the Speaker of the House.

11. If the President is in his room, you must not look in there; you must wait until he is gone before you can open that closed door.

12. Now you will climb the stairs which lead up into the dome. You are high above the city when you have climbed these two hundred and ninety stairs. People walking and riding in the streets are far below you.

13. The broad avenues shaded with trees, and

the many public buildings of different sorts of stone, and the fine homes, make Washington a beautiful city. In the distance are hills and woods and pleasant country houses, and you can see the sun shining on the water of the river.

14. By and by we shall go down to the river, but now we wish to look a little longer at the panorama which is all below us. It is a bird's-eye view of the city that we have now. There are many larger cities than Washington, but this is the capital of the country.

15. Nowhere else in the United States can you see so many great buildings which belong to all the country, and of which everybody has a right to be proud.

16. Look down at the grounds about the Capitol. They are larger than many a farmer's entire farm, and the grounds about the President's house are even larger than these.

17. Yes, you may visit the White House. It is a little more than a mile from the Capitol, and you may walk or ride as you like. You will enjoy looking at the flowers in the

garden, and if it is a public reception day, you may go up the steps and into the house, and see the President and his wife.

18. If you had plenty of time to spend in Washington you could see a great many famous and beautiful pictures in the art galleries of the city. And you may be sure you would never tire of sitting on a bench in the park, during a warm day, and watching the people riding and driving. There are people from all parts of the world living in Washington.

19. They are selected by the governments of other countries to come and live in our capital to help us to be friendly with their people at home. Most of them bring their families with them to Washington. You will see Japanese, French, English, Chinese, and German children, as well as American ones, playing in the Washington parks.

20. Down the river at Mt. Vernon are the home and the tomb of General Washington, the first President, for whom the capital is named.

21. Let us go down to the river. It is called the Potomac, and is a very broad stream. The

story is told that General Washington once threw a dollar from one bank of the Potomac to the other. Of course you will wish to take a stone and try your strength in throwing, but you will not succeed in reaching the middle of the stream.

22. The river grows narrower very soon after one goes a little way up stream from the city. If you should go up the river in a boat, you would find it growing narrower and narrower, until at last it would be such a shallow little stream that your boat would graze on the pebbles and sand in the brook's bed.

23. And if you got out of the boat and walked up the bank of the little stream, following it as far as possible, by-and-by you would come to a spring high up in the mountains.

24. Walk back to your boat and drift down stream again. You would find the mountains giving place to hills. Creeks and brooks and little rivers pouring into the current, make the broad Potomac.

25. You would float back to the boat-landing at Washington, thinking that you knew a good deal about the formation of a river.

26. But what becomes of the great thirsty river, which has been drinking up all of the smaller streams?

CHAPTER II.

A BOAT JOURNEY.

1. As you float down the Potomac River in your imaginary boat, you are perfectly safe. The steamers which come up the stream cannot harm your make-believe craft. And if you look with your mind's eye while reading these pages, you will see many of the things which your real eyes would show you if your boat was a real one. In that case, you would be obliged to spend a great deal of time rowing and looking out for the big steamers.

2. Now you may notice that the stream grows rapidly wider, and that there are many small inlets along its banks. By keeping your boat near one bank of the broad river, you can see how the water has made these inlets, wearing the land into little nooks and scallops along the shores.

3. These inlets are different from the places worn away by the entrance of smaller streams into the river. Those are called the mouths of the streams, while the inlets are worn away by the play of the great river itself on its banks.

4. Something besides the flowing of the water in its regular current has made many of these inlets quite large. This is the action of the water flowing backwards. But you wonder how that can be. Do rivers ever run backwards? Yes; some of the water in the Potomac River and in many other rivers runs up stream twice every day. This takes place only in rivers near the ocean. It is the tide.

5. As you float more and more slowly down the stream, you feel that a great force is holding your boat backwards a little. It is as if some power was making you go more slowly than the river current had been carrying you on. Yet this river current keeps your boat going on and on towards the sea.

6. By and by you see that all the inlets and the little creeks are full and overflowing. If you dip your fingers over the boat's side into the

river, and taste of the water, you will find that it is brackish. It is not really salt, but it is not so fresh and sweet as the water of the spring high up in the mountains.

7. Wait until the tide turns. Drift on in your boat until you come nearer the great arm of the sea called Chesapeake Bay. The inlets in the river bank were like little bays, and Chesapeake Bay is like a big inlet in the coast of the country.

8. The tide is running out, and your boat goes faster and faster down the river towards the bay. The tide pushes you forward now with as much force as awhile ago it held you back.

9. Twice every day the water of the ocean flows a little way up on its shores and a long way up into the rivers, and twice every day the tides flow back again to the ocean.

10. It is low tide as your boat drifts out into Chesapeake Bay. You can see on the shores the line that marks how high the water has been, and you see that the inlets are no longer overflowing with water.

11. It is a long ride that you have had on the Potomac River, coming down to Chesapeake Bay. The mouth of the Potomac is nearly four hundred miles from the place where your boat grated on the pebbles in its shallow head waters. You have come nearly a quarter of the way from Washington with the tide meeting you twice every day and making you go more slowly. Now you must row your boat for seventy-five miles down the bay, before you come out into the open ocean.

12. You remember the little points of land jutting out into the river on both sides of each little inlet? Here are two great points of land, coming out into the sea, one on either side of the entrance to Chesapeake Bay. They are called Cape Charles and Cape Henry; for capes, like rivers, must have names.

13. It has been a long boat journey on the Potomac, but in learning something about this river, you have learned something about all great rivers. You know that they rise from springs in the high lands, in hills or mountains. You have seen how they all come down to the lower lands,

gathering the waters of smaller streams as they come, and growing broader and broader, until at last they reach the salt water of the sea.

14. A river's part in making this world good to live in is a very useful one. When we come to another river later on we will try to see some of the ways in which it may be useful. Now we must look to our oars.

15. After passing Cape Charles and Cape Henry, we are out in the Atlantic Ocean. Chesapeake Bay and its oyster-beds are behind us.

16. Now, if you wish, we will row around to Norfolk and take a steamer going northward, for it would not be pleasant to go up the coast of the Atlantic over the big waves in a row-boat, even an imaginary one.

CHAPTER III.

UP THE COAST.

1. Our steamer has come from the South, and is going to New York. On board are a number of people who have been in Florida.

One gentleman has a case of oranges open near him on the deck, and amuses himself by giving them away to the boys and girls on the steamer. He seems to enjoy talking to his young friends.

2. "These oranges were picked fresh from the trees only a few days ago," he says. "I had the pleasure of putting some of them into this box myself, as soon as they were picked from the tree where they grew. Here is a picture of the orange-grove where I found them.

3. "Orange-growing is a great business in Florida. It is so warm there that the fruit can ripen out of doors during months that are cold in the North. It keeps a great many people busy cultivating the trees, taking care of them, picking and packing the fruit.

4. "Now when *I* was a boy, an orange was a great treat. Once in a long while, at Christmas-time, or on a birthday, children had oranges given them. Most of our oranges in those days came from other countries, — from countries over the ocean. Now it takes all the time of thousands of people in our own country to grow oranges for boys and girls to eat. Probably the

boys and girls eat half of the oranges that grow in Florida."

5. The gentleman takes off his glasses, wipes them carefully, puts them back on his nose, and looks around the deck at his hearers.

A FLORIDA ORANGE-GROVE.

6. "The orange-tree is not a tall tree, nor a very short one," he continues; "its branches do not spread about like the branches of an apple-tree. It isn't a very good tree for climbing, but"

—and the gentleman smiles — " it is a very good tree to stand under when one gets to be too old to climb; for the branches, with the fruit, hang low."

7. When you have looked long enough at the picture of the orange-grove, come to the railing round the deck. As the steamer pushes her way along through the blue waves, you can see a great deal of the shores we are passing; for our make-believe steamer may go nearer the coast than a real one without bringing us into danger of running ashore on a sand-reef.

8. We can see the islands that we pass just as they are. Each one is a piece of the land, with the water all around it. Some of the islands are large and some are small. There are long inlets back of these coast islands.

9. After a time we come to another great bay, extending inward between two points of land. Cape Henlopen and Cape May are on either side of Delaware Bay.

10. In the State of Delaware are fruit-orchards as famous as the orange-groves of Florida. Delaware peaches are as delicious as Florida oranges; and if you wish to see a beautiful

sight, you will go through the Delaware peach-orchards when the trees are all in bloom.

11. Cape Henlopen is on the Delaware side of the bay and Cape May on the northern or New Jersey side. The beach at Cape May is a fine one for bathing, and as we go by in the steamer, we can see on the shore the hotels and cottages where people come to live in the summer and enjoy the sea-air and bathing.

12. We see thousands of these summer homes as we go on up the coast; for Atlantic City and Long Branch are summer-places, too, and very many of the houses in them are closed during the winter months.

13. The shore has been sandy all the way up the Jersey coast. Just before going into New York Bay, we pass a long, low point of land, extending toward the north. It is very sandy, and it is in shape a little like a huge hook; so this cape is called Sandy Hook.

14. The light from the light-house on Sandy Hook can be seen when we are far out upon the ocean. People nearing New York are always glad to see it, for they know their journey is

almost at an end. And no matter how pleasant a journey may have been, it is always pleasant to come to the end of it.

15. As we go up the Narrows and into New York Bay, we see a great many other steamers

BROOKLYN BRIDGE AND THE NARROWS.

large and small, and sailing vessels also from all over the world. Pilot-boats, with their numbers painted on their white sails, come down the bay to guide the ships into port. We pass several islands. Our steamer goes safely among the crowding vessels of all countries to the dock where we are to land.

16. Yonder is a ship loaded with coffee from the far-off island of Java. There is one loaded with lumber from our Western forests, sailing away to England, and there is another in which living cattle and sheep are going away to be turned into food for people in distant homes.

17. It would be interesting to know what every ship in the harbor is loaded with. Then we could realize a little how busy people are everywhere, working to provide food, shelter, and clothing to use for themselves and to sell to one another.

18. Our steamer stops, and we go ashore. We are now in the largest city in America, and one of the most important cities in the world. More than a million people have their homes here. New York carries on an immense trade, which extends not only to all parts of the United States, but to all other nations. We soon find our way through the streets to Broadway.

CHAPTER IV.

IN NEW YORK.

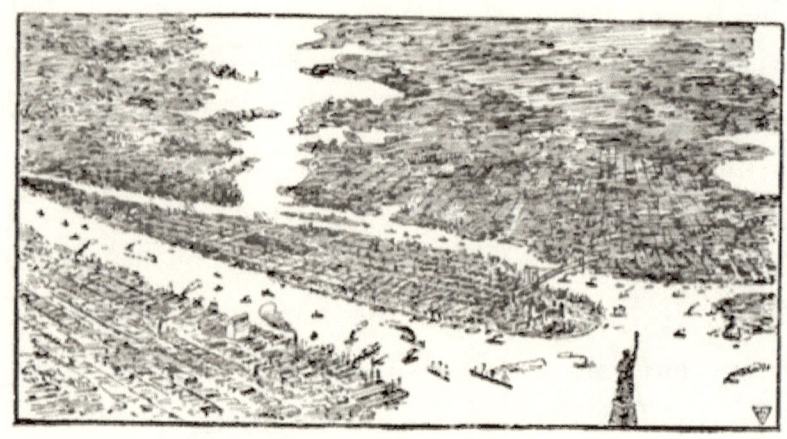

BIRD'S-EYE VIEW OF NEW YORK.

1. Broadway is a long and wide street, full of busy, hurrying people. As you walk along towards the post-office, you pass tall business buildings and hotels, and you hurry across the street to keep out of the way of the cabs and carts and other carriages, which crowd one another more closely than the ships in the bay.

2. You will enjoy standing on the great stone steps of the post-office for a little while. On one side of you is Broadway, full of people. Before you is a small park. There are benches under

the trees, and you may go and sit down there if you like, and watch the hurrying people, as they pass to and fro, each intent upon his special business.

3. Walk along Broadway to Trinity Church. It is a very old church, built long ago, and in the church-yard behind the high iron fence there are many graves. The view from Trinity steeple is worth the trouble of climbing up the stairs; for when you are up there you can see even more than you saw from the dome of the Capitol at Washington.

4. All the city with its thousands of buildings, its churches and its homes, the trains on the elevated railroad flying about the city,—this and much more you can see from Trinity steeple.

5. You must take a ride on the elevated railroad. You go up a long flight of stairs from the street to the railroad track. A little gate is opened for you. The train comes quickly along on its high platform. You go into a car and ride off up town, on a railroad built high up in the air, over the heads of the people in the streets.

6. On your way to Central Park, get out and go down to the ground again at one of the up-town stations. Walk over to Fifth Avenue, and see some of the handsomest homes in New York.

7. You will wish to spend the day in Central Park, and indeed you would need to be there all day if you tried to walk about much. But there are park wagons in which you may ride about, and see the flowers and the fountains and the trees, the carriages of people driving, and the goat-carts with which small boys and girls are amusing themselves.

8. You must have a ride, too, up the River-side drive. On one side of you, as you go, are pleasant homes with fine grounds and trees. On the other side is the Hudson River, with steam-ers coming down from Albany, and bright little boats and yachts with their white sails.

9. When you reach a knoll a few miles above the city, you will see the grave of General Grant. From this knoll, you can see a long way up and down the beautiful Hudson.

10. On the other side of the river, a little dis-tance up the stream, there is a great wall of rock rising straight up from the river bank.

11. This wall of rock is several miles long, and is higher than Trinity steeple. It is called the Palisades of the Hudson, and people come very great distances to see this river-wall with the forest trees growing on the top of it, and the crumbling fragments falling to the bank below.

12. If you should make a journey up the Hudson, you would find that it is not like the Potomac River which you know so well, for the Hudson has come through hills and mountains all the way. The smaller streams which come into it flow more rapidly and over rockier beds than those which came into the Potomac.

13. One of the little rivers that flows into the Hudson has a very useful work to do in supplying the people in the great city of New York with water. This is the Croton River.

14. The water is carried down to the city in an enormous covered trough, called an aqueduct, made for the purpose, and this, in its turn, supplies the pipes for the kitchens, and the bath-rooms, the laundries and the fountains of the city.

15. You may have a drink of Croton water when you go back to town. Most of the cities

in our country are supplied with good water in
some such way.

16. You will not wish to leave New York
without going over the great bridge which
connects this city with Brooklyn. You may walk
over, or go over in a cable car, just as you like.

17. When you are high up on the arch of the
bridge, you see a steamer with its tall pipes
and masts passing down East River beneath
you. In the river below you can see ferry-
boats, too, going back and forth between Brooklyn and New York. These used to be the only
means of crossing from the island on which New
York is built to the island on which Brooklyn
is built. But now the big bridge makes it
easier for the people to go back and forth.

18. If you stop to think now, you can almost
see from what you have learned that New York
is on an island. There is the bay on the south
side of the city, the Hudson River on the west,
and East River on the east side. On the north
is a little creek separating Manhattan Island
from the shore. Look on the map, and you
will see how it is.

19. Come down to the dock again. It is late in the afternoon of a sunshiny summer day. A steamer is waiting there all ready to go to Newport.

CHAPTER V.

TO NEWPORT.

1. Our steamer goes up East River, and under the' Brooklyn bridge, from which we looked down awhile ago. On we sail, and from our place on the deck, we can see the towns and cities clustering so closely about New York and Brooklyn that all seem like one great city whose different parts are called by different names.

2. The island on which Brooklyn is built is a very large and long one, and is south of us all night as we go towards Newport in our steamer berths. It is called Long Island, while the water we are passing over is Long Island Sound. This is salt sea water, and is very deep in many places; still it is not so deep as the ocean. The sound is divided from the ocean by Long Island and the main land is north of it. It has

two openings into the ocean, one through New York Bay, and one at its eastern end.

3. Most sounds are like this one, separated from the ocean by an island. They are not like bays, you see, because a bay goes up into the main land, and has only one opening into the salt water.

4. Early in the morning we land at Newport, one of the capitals of Rhode Island. We have travelled all night on the Sound steamer, and have come safely by Point Judith, a rocky cape, where in storms it is dangerous for passing vessels, and where ships are sometimes wrecked.

5. But in the harbor at Newport, the water is calm and clear. We can go for a walk all about Newport, and have glimpses of the sea at every turn, for this town is on an island, too.

6. It often happens that a city is built on an island because there is a good harbor between the island and the main land.

7. Some people believe that the first ships that landed in our country came to the harbor at Newport hundreds of years before Columbus discovered America. You can see at Newport a

round tower of stone, built very firmly and all
overgrown with ivy.   It is called "The Old Mill."

8. It was standing there when people whose
writings we have
first went to the
place, and was
perhaps built by
Norsemen long
ago. Nobody
can be quite cer-
tain that it was
used for a mill,
and the poet
Longfellow, in
one of his poems,
makes it the
home of a bold Norse sailor and his bride.   Here
is a stanza from the poem, "The Skeleton in
Armor":—

THE OLD MILL.

> 9. "Three weeks we westward bore,
>   And when the storm was o'er,
>   Cloud-like we saw the shore,
>   Stretching to leeward;
>   There for my lady's bower

Built I the lofty tower,
Which to this very hour
Stands looking seaward."

10. You must go for a walk on the Cliffs after looking at the Old Mill. The Cliffs are rocky walls, standing straight up from the sea, as the Palisades rise from the water of the Hudson River. But they are not so high as the Palisades. The pebble you toss down into the water from the walk splashes in the sea before you can count ten, unless you count very fast indeed. Your path is a pleasant one as you stroll around the Cliffs, for they are grassy to the very edge of the rocks.

11. The people who have summer homes at Newport have made their grounds beautiful, and the houses you pass in your walk around this path are all very handsome ones.

12. There is a fine beach for bathing; and if you wait until ten or eleven o'clock in the forenoon, you will have a gay bathing scene before you, for then numbers of people, young and old, come down for their morning dip in the sea. Later in the day there is a great deal of driv-

ing on Bellevue Avenue, and you see fine carriages and horses, as the people drive up and
down.

13. Newport is a city of pleasure, and full of
beautiful summer homes. Our steamer now takes
us to Fall River, which is a working town. The
people here are nearly all very busy; and the little
rapid river that supplies power to run the mills, in
which many of the people work, is busy too. You
have seen several ways in which a river may be
useful. Here at Fall River you see one helping
to make calicoes by its work in the mills.

14. You walk through one of the mills where
calicoes are woven, and made ready for the stamp-
ing of the patterns by the print-works. In the
first great room are huge bales of cotton brought
from the Southern States. In other rooms people
are picking, carding, and working at the looms.
The process of manufacture goes on until the
packages of cotton cloth are folded, ready for the
printing.

15. There is a mill for making ginghams, and
a woollen mill, also, in this busy town. People in
distant countries, as well as people in our own

country, wear clothes made of cloth manufactured in Fall River.

16. Above the town is a large and lovely lake from which a swift little river runs down to the bay. You could not take a boat journey on this stream, for it plunges down the steep hill at a rapid rate.

17. At one place in the town the river quite disappears for a distance, and now public buildings stand on made land, above the hidden river.

18. Further up the bay, as far as steamers can go, on an arm of the bay called the Narragansett River, is the city of Providence, the other capital of Rhode Island. It is a city of hills, and on these hills are many pleasant homes.

19. In the business part of the town is an arcade, a long, covered archway from which open a great number of stores and shops. There are very few arcades in our American cities, although they are quite common in the cities of Europe.

20. Brown University and the State Normal School are here, and the city is noted for its fine academies and other schools.

CHAPTER VI.

IN BOSTON.

1. We are now going to Boston. Look on the map and see how short the journey is by the railroad. It would take a long time, even if the steamer went very fast, to go from Fall River down past the islands of Martha's Vineyard and Nantucket, and around Cape Cod to Boston. See on the map how long and narrow this cape is.

2. The waves of the ocean and the waves of the bay have been washing away the sandy land for hundreds of years. Cape Cod looks very narrow on the map, but it is a strip of land wide enough for farms, towns, and villages.

3. There are many acres of cranberry marshes on Cape Cod; and the bright berries, picked in their season by old and young, are sent away in boxes and barrels, to be served with roast turkey at thousands of dinner-tables, east and west.

4. The train which takes you to Boston goes through a pleasant country. There are farms

with small fields, and towns with many white
houses, and there are woods, hills, and clear running streams.

5. As we near the city, the towns and villages
are closer together, and for several miles before
coming into Boston we pass through beautiful suburban towns.   Many men who have homes in
these suburbs go into the city for business every
day.   It is said that no other city has so many
pleasant country places within ten miles of its
business centre.   Up and down the shores of the
bay, by the lakes, and in the groves which surround the city, — everywhere are beautiful homes.

6. Boston's business streets are not so straight,
broad, and handsome as those of Washington and
New York; but you need not go, at your first
visit, to the narrow and picturesque streets found
in the business part of the city.

7. As you come out of the station, you see
two cars approaching quite rapidly.   Beckon, and
the man who manages the motor will stop these
electric cars.   Get in and you will be whizzed
along past pleasant homes and beautiful churches,
through wide streets and roads, then slowly by

an easy grade up a long hill. On top of this hill is a great reservoir fed by pipes from Lake Cochituate; from this reservoir the city receives most of its water supply.

8. On your way back into town, you may, if you like, stop the car at Beacon Street and walk over Beacon Hill. As you go along the street, you catch glimpses, now and then, at cross streets, of a broad lake-like sheet of water back of the houses on your left. This is called the Back Bay.

9. Once the water of this inner bay extended to the very place where you are now walking, and even still farther inland. More ground was needed, on which to build houses in this part of the city, and the water was shallow on this side of the bay. So at an expense of much labor and money, a great stretch of land was made, by filling up this side of the bay with earth brought from outside the city. On this made land the newer and broader streets of the city have been laid out.

10. You walk on and pass the Public Garden, brilliant with flowers and foliage. As you go on up the hill you pass the Common. This is a

grassy park of more than forty acres, shaded
with noble old elm trees — the pride of all
Bostonians. This is at your right hand, and at

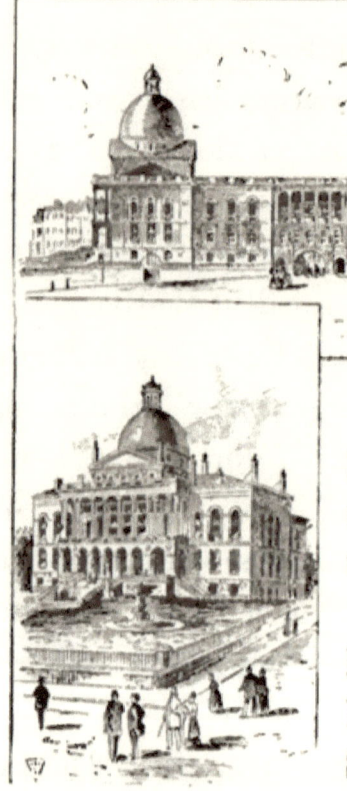

THE NEW EXTENSION.

your left are high houses,
older than those on the
made land.

11. On top of Beacon
Hill is the State House.
It is the capitol of the
State of Massachusetts,
and its dome is gilded so

THE STATE HOUSE.

that it shines and glimmers in the sunlight.
Whenever you go into the suburbs of Boston,
you can see from far away that big, bright,
gilded dome shining on the top of Beacon Hill.

An extension is soon to be added to the State House. and the picture shows how it will look when the architect's plans are carried out and the building is completed.

12. Boston is often spoken of as "the Hub." This nickname was given to it many years ago. Dr. Oliver Wendell Holmes, one of the most famous of the many literary men who have lived near Beacon Hill, wrote in one of his books, "Boston State House is the hub of the universe."

13. The hub of a wheel is its central part, you know, and Boston has been noted as the centre of learning in our country. There are many great colleges and libraries in and near the city; and although books are now written and published in every large city in the United States, many of our first great writers lived near Boston, and the city has become celebrated for the literary taste of its people.

14. To your bird's-eye views of other cities of our country, you must add the out-look from the lantern above the dome of the State House. When you have climbed up to this point of view, you can see a fine panorama. On the east

is Boston harbor, dotted with islands, and opening into Massachusetts Bay. You can see the
masts of many vessels, and there is a great
ocean steamer just leaving Boston Harbor. You
have glimpses of the water of the Charles River
flowing through Cambridge and other towns at
the west.

15. You can also see the tower of Memorial

THE HOME OF LONGFELLOW.

Hall at Harvard College. Not far from the college is the Longfellow home, the "Craigie House,"
where the poet lived and died, and where General
Washington once lived for a short time.

16. Look towards the north and see the Monument on Bunker Hill in Charlestown, a lofty monument of granite, to mark the spot where an important battle was once fought,— the battle of Bunker Hill. As you look towards the south, the city is spread out as in a picture. The Common lies in front of you just beyond Beacon Street.. You can almost imagine yourself walking on the tops of those thickly spreading elm branches.

17. Beyond and to the left are high business buildings, depots, factories, hotels, stores, and offices; and to the right are rows of city dwellings, reaching far away towards a long low range of hills called the Blue Hills.

18. Come down the State House steps and walk from Beacon Hill to Washington Street. You pass the fountains and statues in the grounds of the State House. The grass is always green on this sunny hill quite early in the spring.

19. Along the street a short distance is the Athenæum, a library building where there are also some fine pictures. A little farther down

the hill rises the tall tower of the Parker House.
On your way to Washington Street you go across
Tremont Street and down School Street past the
City Hall.

20. Narrow Washington Street, with its high
buildings, is one of the chief business streets of
the city. Within a short distance of each other
are the Old South Meeting-House and the Old
State House. Just around the corner from the
meeting-house door is a building marked with a
tablet saying that here Benjamin Franklin was
born.

21. A short walk through the winding streets,
and you will come to Faneuil Hall, which is
called the Cradle of Liberty. In the early times,
when our forefathers wished to make this
country independent of England, it was their
custom to meet in this hall. The hall is
still used for public meetings. The lower part of
the building is now a market for vegetables,
fruits, and the like. On every hand, in Boston,
you can see something interesting which has to
do with the story of our country.

22. You will like to cross Charlestown

bridge and go out for a ride on the Medford road, the one that Paul Revere took,

"On the eighteenth of April in seventy-five."

From the bridge you can see the tower of the old North Church, of which the poet has sung,

"He said to his friend, 'If the British march
By land or sea from the town to-night,
Hang a lantern aloft in the belfry arch
Of the North Church tower as a signal light, —
One if by land, and two if by sea,
And I on the opposite shore will be
Ready to ride and spread the alarm
Through every Middlesex village and farm
For the country folk to be up and to arm.'"

CHAPTER VII.

NEW ENGLAND.

1. Six of the United States form a part of our country called New England. Boston is the largest city and the capital of the State of Massachusetts. Maine is the largest New England State, and Rhode Island is the smallest.

2. You have already been in the little State of Rhode Island, while visiting Newport and Providence. The other New England States are Connecticut, Vermont, and New Hampshire.

3. In each of these States there are many mills and factories, not only for making cotton and woollen cloths, but also for making paper, boots and shoes, steam-engines, straw-hats, chairs and tables, and indeed almost everything one can think of.

4. One of the reasons that so many people in New England are busy in manufacturing is this: The farms of this part of the country are not large enough, nor is the soil rich enough, to grow grain and fruit, and cattle and sheep, to feed the people here. So they make things which they can sell to the people in the West, where there are larger and richer farms than in New England.

5. Still there are many good farms in these States, even in the rough parts of the country; and there are many hills and mountains here.

6. When several mountains stand together in a line, we call them a chain of mountains. Some of

the high points of land may extend further up towards the sky than others; these are called peaks. A boy who had never seen the mountains once asked his teacher if people could see their tops.

7. There is no mountain in the world so high that one has any difficulty in seeing the top of it, unless indeed the clouds are hanging low about the peak. But it would take the boy a long time to walk to the top of any high mountain in New England.

8. In the State of Vermont there is a range called the Green Mountains. There is much fine marble quarried in Vermont; slate is found there, and made into the slates used at school. There is marble in New Hampshire, too, and also strong and beautiful granite, which is used for buildings in many towns far and near.

9. There is a chain of mountains in New Hampshire, called the White Mountains, celebrated for their grandeur and beauty. A large number of people visit the White Mountains every summer to enjoy the fine views and breathe the pure air on the heights. These

IN THE WHITE MOUNTAINS.

mountains are in two groups separated by a high plain.

10. A large plain of this sort is sometimes called a plateau. The openings between the mountains

are notches. Franconia Notch is one of the most beautiful of these mountain gateways. Standing on the porch of a house at Franconia, one may see long, lovely reaches of mountain and valley.

11. In the early autumn the frosts make the maples and oaks on the mountain sides gorgeous with color, while in the valleys below the trees are still green. The mountains, late in September, are like great bright bouquets, and the foliage of the trees shows off brilliantly against the clear, deep blue of the sky.

12. Mount Washington is the highest peak in this group. There is a very steep railroad going up to the look-out on the top. You would be very likely to close your eyes to keep yourself from growing dizzy should the mountain engine take you up the precipitous incline.

13. The coast of New England has many fine harbors, where vessels carrying goods and passengers back and forth may land, and be loaded, or unloaded.

14. All along the coast from Cape Cod to Passamaquoddy Bay, which is at the most eastern part of our country, the business of fishing is

carried on.   Our fishing-vessels sometimes go further still, even as far as the banks of Newfound-
land ; but there is a vast amount of fish caught
in the waters off our own coast.

A MOUNTAIN VALLEY.

15. From the headland at Nahant, where sailors
say the sea-serpent sometimes comes, a fisherman
might sail his boat down to the rocks of Cape
Ann, where millions of wild roses bloom.   If he
caught only a few fishes of each kind found in

these waters, he would have a load before his trip was done.

16. Imagine him as he goes past the islands of Boston Harbor with the sun shining on the white sails of his boat. He steers safely through the straits, and on towards the promontory of Nahant. He passes Revere Beach, a long way off, and skirts the sandy shores and the high cliffs of Nahant.

17. The fisherman's boat goes on. He can see the narrow neck of land that separates the bay on which he rides from Lynn Harbor. This neck of land, or isthmus, goes out from the mainland to the Nahant headland. There is a fine drive along the beautiful beach.

18. Beyond is Lynn Harbor, in which may be seen the masts of many ships which have entered the quiet water.

19. He comes to another fine harbor at Marblehead, where his boat will be safe, no matter how terrible a storm may rage outside. The people at Marblehead have been fishermen for hundreds of years. It is said that the children there know more about the fishing business than most grown people elsewhere.

20. On goes the fishing-boat; it sails in and out of the harbor of Salem. This is the city where people were hung for witches a long time ago. Here may be seen the sails of beautiful, fast-sailing yachts. Here is situated one of the State Normal Schools of Massachusetts.

21. On sails the boat, past the rocks at Manchester, and the sandy shore where the waves make such music that it is called "the singing beach." Farther still on the North Shore, near the pleasant town of Magnolia, is a dangerous reef of rocks, a little way out in the sea. It is called the reef of Norman's Woe.

22. In the sunshine on a bright day the "white and fleecy waves" breaking over the rocks look "soft as carded wool." But when there is a storm, this reef of Norman's Woe is very dangerous. Here was the wreck of the schooner *Hesperus*, of which you have read in the ballad by Longfellow.

23. " Colder and colder blew the wind,
         A gale from the northeast,
      The snow fell hissing in the brine,
         And the billows frothed like yeast.

"And fast through the midnight dark and drear,
  Through the whistling sleet and snow,
Like a sheeted ghost, the vessel swept
  Towards the reef of Norman's Woe."

24. You remember how the skipper bound his little daughter to the mast, and wrapped her warm in his coat before he died of the bitter cold, and how the little girl, too, was drowned.

"The salt sea was frozen on her breast,
  The salt tears in her eyes."

25. Our fisherman sails on past the beautiful bay at Gloucester, where he sees the sunset light glowing on the water; still he goes on, and at night casts anchor in a quiet cove on the coast of Cape Ann. One of the poems of Whittier about Cape Ann begins : —

" From the hills of home, forth looking, far beneath the
    tent-like span
  Of the sky, I see the white gleam of the headland of
    Cape Ann.
  Well I know its coves and beaches to the ebb-tide glim-
    mering down,
  And the white-walled hamlet children of its ancient fish-
    ing-town."

CHAPTER VIII.

MORE ABOUT NEW ENGLAND.

1. The Merrimac River comes down to the sea at the pleasant old town of Newburyport. The Merrimac is one of the busiest of all the useful rivers of New England. In order to use the water-power furnished by this river many mills and factories have been built along its banks.

2. It is a rapid river, and at the cities of Lowell and Manchester there are falls which add much to its power. Lawrence, Nashua, and Concord are other important towns on the banks of the Merrimac.

3. You can scarcely think of a thing that is not manufactured in some one of these places. Pins and pumps, machinery and medicines, toys and tools, shoes, locomotives, and carriages, as well as all sorts of cloths, are made in the mills on the Merrimac.

4. You cannot imagine the miles of cotton cloth and prints made here. One mill alone can make enough gingham in a day to give two or three

thousand girls each a new dress. And with all the gingham mills going, you would think everybody in the world would have to wear nothing but gingham, in order to use it all up. But you would think the same when you saw the great piles of woollen cloths and calicoes ready to be sent away.

5. Yet there are people to buy everything that is made; and the men who own the mills do all that they can to improve the machinery and obtain better workmen and workwomen, so that the mills can produce things faster, and thus supply the demand.

6. Concord is the capital of New Hampshire. If you were in Concord, and should go on the train from there to Montpelier, the capital of Vermont, on your way you would cross a river much wider and longer than the Merrimac. This is the Connecticut River. It separates the State of New Hampshire from Vermont, then flows southward a long way, through the States of Massachusetts and Connecticut, till at last it reaches the salt water of Long Island Sound.

7. Once upon a time there was a boy who lived

on the banks of the Connecticut River, in a city named Hartford, which you can easily find on the map. This boy had studied geography; and he knew that the map of the State of Vermont, the "Green Mountain State," is often colored green. And he had the notion in his head that the country in Vermont was greener than in Connecticut, and that it would look a good deal like the map.

8. It came about in time that he went with his father to pay a visit to an aunt who lived in Vermont. It was winter, and the ground was all covered with snow. The Green Mountains were as white as the hills near his home, or as Mount Tom and Mount Holyoke, which he had passed while coming across Massachusetts in the cars.

9. "Well, well, well!" exclaimed the boy, "Vermont doesn't look a bit like the map! It's the same color as Connecticut."

10. Maps are very good things to give one an idea of the relations between different parts of .the country; but when you look at the long, dark line on the map, marked "Connecticut River," you should think of a broad and beautiful river,

the longest of all in New England. You would find very many mills in a journey down this "long river." That is the meaning of its Indian name.

11. Most boys would wish to visit a town named Waterbury, which is on another river in the western part of the state.

12. Can you tell why?

13. At New Haven you would see the buildings of Yale College, and walk under the branches of beautiful elm trees. New Haven is called "The City of Elms."

14. You have been wandering about a little in every one of the New England States, except Maine. You have seen that they all have a sea-coast, except Vermont. The coast of New Hampshire is not very extensive, but on it is situated the city of Portsmouth.

15. Then comes the coast of Maine, extending for hundreds of miles, with bays, inlets, coves, and river-mouths, and more beautiful islands than have ever been counted. Our fisherman would find salmon in the Penobscot and the Kennebec rivers; and he would find logs for lumber floating on these rivers. In the winter a great deal

of ice is cut on the Maine rivers and lakes for
the use of people in many different places.

16. Up in the great forests of Maine, men are
busy every winter cutting
down trees for lumber, and
the rivers carry the logs
for them down to the
towns and the ships.

You understand
now, too, some of
the reasons why
large towns are al-
most always built on or near rivers. Portland
and Bangor are among the large and important
towns in the State of Maine.

17. Portland has a beautiful harbor. Augusta

is the capital of Maine. Mount Desert Island is a famous summer resort. People come to the Maine coast and the Maine woods in summer from towns very far away.

18. Passamaquoddy Bay is the most easterly bay in our country; beyond, both land and water belong to another nation. The water near the shore is owned by the country that owns the land. The open ocean, of course, belongs to everybody; but each government must look after and maintain the rights of fishermen near its own shores.

CHAPTER IX.

FROM LAKE CHAMPLAIN TO PITTSBURG.

1. Between the Green Mountains of Vermont and the Adirondack Mountains of New York lies a beautiful lake called Lake Champlain. The name was given to it in honor of a French traveller who explored this wild northern country hundreds of years ago, before any white people had found homes in New England.

2. This lake has very clear and sparkling water.

BURLINGTON ON LAKE CHAMPLAIN.

and it is dotted over with wooded islands. From either shore you can see in the distance the forest-covered mountains. The city of Burlington is situated near this lake. It is noted for the beauty of the surrounding scenery and for its excellent university.

3. There is a smaller lake, noted for its lovely scenery, at the upper end of Lake Champlain. This is Lake George. If you look for it on the map you will find that it lies at the southern end of Lake Champlain. This is the upper end of the lake, for the water flows towards the north here, instead of towards the south, as in the Hudson River, which is not far from Lake George.

4. There is an elevation of land which divides the streams that flow into Lake George and Lake Champlain from those flowing down towards the Hudson. If you should stand on a high mountain in the Adirondacks, you would see the streams on one side of you flowing north and east towards Lake Champlain, while those on the other side flow south towards the Hudson.

5. The Adirondacks are covered with forests,

and in almost every little valley is a small lake There are few farms and villages in these mountains. It is too wild and rugged for farm and home life, but in the summer there are many camping parties here. At this time of year the hotels near the mountains are full of visitors.

6. People come great distances to hunt in these mountains, and to fish in the mountain streams. Iron ore is found here. It is taken out of the mines and carried to towns in the valleys, where it is made into many useful things.

7. South of the Adirondacks, on a railroad north of Albany, is the famous town of Saratoga. If you should pay a visit to Saratoga, you would very likely spend a morning in going from spring to spring to taste the waters, and in trying to decide which one you liked best.

8. These waters are considered good for various diseases, but people who have no illness go to Saratoga for amusement in the summer season. Nearly every house in Saratoga has a wide piazza, and fine carriages and gayly dressed people are to be seen in the streets all summer long. Not far away, at Mount McGregor, is the cottage

where General Grant died. The house is much visited by tourists to the springs.

9. Albany, the capital of the State of New York, is on the Hudson River. Here are the very steamers which you saw leaving the city of New York to come up the Hudson, when you were looking at the Palisades. Here is the large and splendid new Capitol upon which workmen have been busy for years, and it is not yet finished.

ON THE ERIE CANAL.

10. The Erie Canal comes into a great basin at Albany. You have imagined yourself travelling on boats, steamers, and railroad trains. Suppose you take the canal-boat at Albany for a short trip.

11. People do not usually care to travel on canal-

boats; they go too slowly. They are used chiefly for carrying grain and lumber. An immense quantity of grain comes to Albany from the West, by way of the Erie Canal. This is a very important water course.

12. But as there is no current to hasten the boats, and as they are towed along by horses or mules that walk on a path by the side of the canal, you can imagine that everybody employed about a canal-boat acts as if he had plenty of time. Very often an entire family makes its home on the boat, and their floating house travels slowly back and forth with them.

13. A canal is always made on fairly level ground; but whenever the land slopes much, the canal-boats are taken up and down by means of gates called locks. You will enjoy watching your boat as it goes up through a lock.

14. When you come to the first lock in this quiet stream, this "home-made river," — for so a bright boy once called the Erie Canal, — you will notice that there are two sets of gates in it, the upper and the lower.

15. In going up the canal your boat enters the

lower gate, which is opened for you by the man who tends the lock. Then he closes the gate behind you, and opens some valves in the upper gate. Slowly, slowly the water runs down into the basin in which your boat is floating.

16. As the water fills the basin, the boat rises higher and higher, until it is on a level with the water beyond the upper gate. Then this gate is swung open; the boy on shore who is driving your tow-mules hits one of them with his stick. They walk forward, and your boat is pulled along by the tow-ropes into the water above the lock.

17. Be careful when you go under a bridge. Don't climb up on any piled-up merchandise, or you may get your hat knocked off. The pretty white bridges over the Erie Canal are a pleasant part of the landscape in New York.

18. Boys and girls travelling by the Erie Railroad on a fast train sometimes amuse themselves by counting the bridges. They do not find them so numerous as the telegraph poles.

19. There are many fine farms in the country through which the Erie Canal is made. The land is rich and fertile all the way to Buffalo. Fruits

and grain, vegetables, cheese, and butter are sent from these farms in great abundance to the towns and cities.

20. When you think of all the people in the city of New York, you can imagine that they must need a great deal of butter for their bread. Much of it is made on the dairy farms of Western New York.

21. After you have had your short ride on the canal-boat, you can take a train at Albany, and enjoy a journey through the fine scenery of the Catskill Mountains. These mountains are not so wild and rugged as the Adirondacks. There are many pleasant homes and pretty villages to be seen from your car-window.

22. By and by your train crosses a railroad bridge over the Susquehanna River. Then for a long time the railroad follows the river valley in the mountains of Pennsylvania. Sometimes the train is on one side of the river, sometimes on the other; it goes wherever it has been the easiest to make the railroad-bed. You cross and recross the river several times.

23. At Wilkesbarre you are in the great coal

and iron mining region of Eastern Pennsylvania. Scranton, another place famous for coal and iron, is not far away. You must stop here, and go about among the mountains to see the coal-mining. Some of the coal is in thick layers near the top of the ground, or on the side of a mountain.

You see men chopping it off, as if they were picking bits off the side of a huge fruit cake.

24. In other places, the coal is deep down in the ground. You go down into one of

IN A COAL MINE.

these mines through a shaft sunk like a well into the ground. There is a platform like a big bucket in the shaft, and on this you may go down, down into the mine.

25. It is an odd feeling that comes over you as

you find yourself sinking down away from the daylight; and you are very likely to take fast hold of the person next to you, as if to keep yourself from falling. When you get well into the mine, you see the little rooms and galleries dug out into the coal veins on every side of the main shaft.

26. The men are working by the light of safety lanterns, hung against the walls and ceilings. Perhaps one of the men will let you take his pick, and break off a bit of the hard coal to take home with you from the mine.

27. The west branch of the Susquehanna joins the main river some distance further down. It is, indeed, a noble and beautiful river that your train follows on its way to Harrisburg, the capital of Pennsylvania. Here also many of the people are busy in the manufacturing of iron and in the shipping of coal.

28. All through this region of the Alleghany Mountains there are wonderful veins of fine hard coal and good iron ore. This iron ore is very black, and looks like dark, rough stone. But when it is melted in the furnaces, it is changed

into iron, from which all sorts of useful things may be made, from the hull of an ocean steamer to a tiny carpet tack.

29. From Harrisburg, westward through Pennsylvania, your train goes through a mountainous country, following for a long distance the river valley of the "blue Juniata." This stream winds about even more than the Susquehanna, and you cross it on bridges many times.

30. The men who made the railroad built it along the river valley, for it was much easier to do so than to build it over the high mountains; but they found it necessary to make a great number of bridges over the Juniata for the railroad.

31. You cross many ranges of the Alleghany Mountains on the way from Harrisburg to Pittsburg. They are all part of the Appalachian mountain system. We call a great number of mountain ranges taken together a mountain system. Some of the ranges of the Alleghanies have very pretty names. We cross the Blue Ridge and Laurel Ridge on our way to Pittsburg.

32. This city has many mills and furnaces. The great, heavy, noisy machinery is at work night and day, and the smoke is always pouring out of the high chimneys. At night we can see flames coming out of the chimneys too, and breaking into sparks that fly about in the dark air like small, glittering stars.

33. The city of Pittsburg is built at a place where two rivers flowing down from the mountains join to form the Ohio River. The mountains that we have crossed make an extensive watershed, as you can easily see by looking on the map. The Ohio River cannot possibly flow towards the Atlantic Ocean, or into one of the bays of the Atlantic, like the other great rivers that we have seen. The coal and iron that are put on the Ohio River steamers go westward through a country quite different from any we have yet seen. In this part of Pennsylvania there are many fine farms.

34. North of Pittsburg is the famous oil region. Many years ago the Indians used to collect small quantities of oil on the shores of streams and sell it for a medicine. People had burned an

oil very much like it in their lamps, which was made from coal, and called coal-oil.

35. Two men from New Haven came to this country and began drilling oil-wells, thinking this natural oil, or petroleum, would be good to burn. It was found that the earth was full of oil-springs; and wells were drilled, and pumps put in at once. Great quantities of oil have been pumped up from these oil-wells since.

CHAPTER X.

THREE CITIES.

1. Philadelphia is the largest city in Pennsylvania. To reach it from Pittsburg, you would be obliged to travel back over the Alleghany Mountains, and through the capital city, Harrisburg. Philadelphia is in the southeastern part of the state.

2. Across the Delaware River, on whose bank it stands, is the state of New Jersey, a country of fruits, flowers, and vegetables. Only a little way to the south, the Delaware River empties into

Delaware Bay. You remember passing the mouth of that bay, and Cape May and Cape Henlopen, on your journey up the Atlantic coast. You are, you see, back now where the rivers flow east towards the Atlantic, not west, like the Ohio River at Pittsburg.

3. In the year 1876 thousands and thousands of people visited Philadelphia. Our country had then been free

INDEPENDENCE HALL.

and independent just one hundred years, and there was a great fair called The Centennial Exposition, held in Fairmount Park at Philadelphia, to celebrate the hundredth anniversary of our freedom.

Americans love freedom. and this is the reason
why the great Exposition in 1876 was held at
Philadelphia.

4. Very many of the visitors to Philadelphia
that year went to the old State House, or Independence Hall, to see the bell, which is one of the
first things you will wish to see—the bell which
was rung when the Declaration of Independence
was signed.

5. If you were in Philadelphia on the Fourth
of July, it would be pleasant to visit Independence Hall, and see this old bell which began
the noise of our national celebration that boys
and girls, and older people too, have been keeping
up every Fourth of July for more than a hundred
years. Do you think the time will ever come
when there will be no celebration of our national
freedom on the Fourth of July?

6. After seeing the bell, you would like to take
a walk through the streets of the city. Near
Independence Hall, in State House Row, are a
number of other very old buildings; none of these
are used for offices. In front of them is a broad
pavement shaded with trees. Whichever way

you walk you are sure to come to a pretty, shady square, like a small park. Franklin Square has a large fountain in it.

7. Although Philadelphia is a large city, one of the largest in our country, it is not so noisy, and the people do not seem in so much of a hurry as in New York. It is a city of homes. Many of them are built of

LAUNCHING A SHIP.

brick; and in this pleasant city of Philadelphia there are very few great tenement houses where people are crowded together too close for comfort.

8. Go down to the wharves, and you will see a great many vessels, loading with coal which has been brought down from the mountains. There is a great ship-yard at Kensington, near Philadelphia. Here and at other places near by great ships and steamers are built and launched. It is interesting and exciting to see a new steamer, or a ship, let down into the water for the first time.

9. From Philadelphia to Baltimore, in Maryland, is a pleasant ride by train along the upper shores of Chesapeake Bay. Your boat journey in this great bay has made you remember its name. But Baltimore is a long way north of the mouth of the Potomac River, where your boat entered the bay. And as you went southward, you did not come near the oyster-beds of this part of the Chesapeake. Oysters, as you know, are found in the water instead of on land. They are usually found in shallow water, on the sandy bottoms, or clinging to rocks under the water.

10. Oysters are taken out by millions from the Chesapeake Bay. Great quantities of them are put into tin cans in Baltimore, sealed up, and sent to places where fresh oysters cannot be sent. But

they can be sent fresh to many places a long way inland.

11. Peaches and strawberries grow plentifully in the country about Baltimore. Many people in the city are employed in canning these fruits, so you see that oysters are not the only things canned in Baltimore.

12. Outside the city are the Bare Hills. where iron ore is found. You can see these from Federal Hill, a pleasant outlook above the harbor. From your outlook here you can see the ships and the city, the great cross-shaped church,—the Cathedral, — and a fine column of white marble, a monument to General Washington. A great many of the buildings in the city are made of Baltimore marble, found in quarries not far away.

13. A beautiful yellow bird, the oriole, which you may have seen, is sometimes called the Baltimore oriole. You are likely to see some of them in the groves of Maryland. They are graceful, lively little creatures, yellow as sunshine, and gifted with a sweet song of several notes, like a musical call. They build odd, bag-like nests, which hang to the branches of trees; so

they are sometimes called hang-birds. They spend the winter in Mexico or some other far southern country, and come northward in the summer-time.

14. Annapolis, the capital of Maryland, is farther down the shores of the bay. There is a fine naval academy in Annapolis, where young men go to be trained for service on our ships of war.

15. You will be surprised by looking at the map to see how nearly you have wandered back to Washington, the capital of our country, in the District of Columbia, which is next to the state of Maryland. The climate is warm in this state, and tobacco is grown on many of the plantations.

16. Whittier describes the beauty of the fruitful Maryland country in the poem of " Barbara Frietchie." On the map you will find the town of Frederick some distance west of Baltimore.

"Up from the meadows rich with corn,
    Clear in the cool September morn,
    The clustered spires of Frederick stand,
    Green-walled by the hills of Maryland;
    Round about them orchards sweep,
    Apple and peach tree, fruited deep,
    Fair as a garden of the Lord."

CHAPTER XI.

LAKE ONTARIO AND NIAGARA.

1. If you should travel directly westward from the most northern waters of Lake Champlain, you would go, for about eighty miles, on the northern boundary line between our country and Canada. The state of New York is south, and Canada is north, of this boundary line.

2. Nature has separated us from the country north of ours in many places by rivers and lakes, but here the governments long ago decided upon a line. It is a dotted line on the map. It is nothing at all when you come to travel along it. There is no high fence to divide Northern New York from Canada, but the division is well known to the people there.

3. Perhaps there is no fence between your yard and that of your next-door neighbor. It may be that each of you have a lawn, but both of you know how far your land goes. You can easily stand upon the line which has been decided upon, and say, " Our land comes thus far."

4. So with our country. How far north our land here reaches is shown by the line dotted on the map as the northern boundary of New York. For about one hundred miles on the northeastern boundary flows one of the broadest rivers in the world, the St. Lawrence. There are many hundred miles of this great river in Canada, but we will not study any part of it except the part which touches our own country.

5. If we take a steamer at Ogdensburg, and go up the river to Lake Ontario, we shall pass a great number of islands. Remember that we are going up the river, although it is down the map. As the steamer winds its way among the picturesque Thousand Islands, you see on many of the islands pretty houses where people have their summer homes. On some of the larger ones are large hotels. Some of the islands are so tiny that there is only room for the tent of some lonely fisherman. Others have lawns and gardens, and everywhere are boat-houses; and wherever there is a bit of beach, bath-houses, too.

6. The St. Lawrence is so wide here that it seems more like a lake than a river; but if

you throw a leaf or a stick overboard, you will see that it floats slowly away on the current, and towards the northeast.

7. After a time your steamer comes out upon Lake Ontario, the most eastern and the smallest of the five Great Lakes north of the United States. Your steamer is soon out of sight of land. You are out in the middle of the great lake. You might think that you were on the sea, but the little waves made by the steamer as it passes swiftly along break apart at once, and do not look so frothy and so much like soap-suds as salt water does. The water in the Great Lakes is fresh and clear. Lake Ontario is very deep indeed, and on a fine day the water is as blue as the sky.

8. At the town of Oswego, in New York, our steamer stops for a short time. Here is the mouth of the Oswego River, which flows northward down to Lake Ontario from a chain of small lakes in the interior of the state. The Oswego River is the outlet of a number of these small lakes.

9. Our next stop is at Rochester, another city

in the state of New York; here the Genesee
River flows into Lake Ontario.

10. Then we go on towards the Niagara
River; but when we come near the place where
this deep and narrow river comes into Lake
Ontario, our steamer turns one side.

11. Why is it? Why does not the steamer go
up the Niagara River on the way to Lake Erie?
Because it is quite impossible for a steamer to go
up this rushing, rapid river, with its whirlpool
and its mighty falls; but there is a canal between Lake Ontario and Lake Erie. The Welland Canal, which is made, in part, of the
Welland River, is broad enough and deep enough
for these lake steamers to pass through.

12. When we come to the falls, we find a
small steamer which goes about in the broad
basin below the falls, and sails indeed in the
mist and the spray, close to the great tumbling
mass of water. This small steamer is called
the Maid of the Mist.

13. Your first view of Niagara, as you come
from the town, is a confused sight of a great
wide roaring river, falling down banks as high

as hills in half a dozen big waterfalls. But if you get into a cable-car which climbs up and down the steep bank beside the American fall, and ride down, and set out upon the slippery, mossy rocks at the side of the river below this great fall, you will begin to get over your confusion, and to enjoy the wonderful waterfall.

14. You may wish to shut your eyes riding down that steep bank in the cable-car, and you must be careful, after you get out of it, not to slip upon the stones wet with spray from the fall. You look up and see the white water coming down close beside you. It is blue a little way down stream, and deepens into green still farther down, between the rocky walls; but the water of the fall is sparkling and white as it pours down from the height above.

15. The Maid of the Mist comes up to a platform not far away. You go on board. Oil-cloth cloaks and hoods are given you to protect your clothes and hat, and the little steamer puffs away up the stream towards the Canadian falls across the river. The spray blows into your faces, and you hold fast to one another, standing on the

deck, as you go past rocks in the stream, over which the water is breaking into foam. Near a big rock well up to the foot of the falls, across the river, the Maid of the Mist turns around for her return journey.

16. You can see people who have been through the Cave of the Winds, which is under one of the smaller falls, standing on the slippery platform built out on the rocks in front of it. They, too, are dressed in oil-cloth suits; and there are rainbows dancing all around them, as they follow their guide carefully back through the spray to the shore again. The great horseshoe-shaped Canadian fall is now behind you.

17. Your steamer stops for a moment on the Canadian side, then takes you back to the platform where you stepped aboard. You ride up the high, steep bank in the cable-car again, and walk by pleasant paths up to the bridges which lead out to the islands in the middle of the river, just at the edge of the falls.

18. The river is about three-quarters of a mile wide above these islands, just before it divides to form the falls. The water under the bridges is

NIAGARA FALLS.

extremely swift. As you pass over, you toss a stick into the current, and it is whirled away and over the falls, almost before you can catch your breath.

19. On one of the islands you can sit on the shore and reach your hand into the water just where it begins its plunge over the great fall, while you look into the seething pool far below you. Between the furthest of the islands the water seems to be boiling, so wildly is it foaming and hurrying towards the fall.

20. There is a story of a lady who came out on these islands with her husband, and becoming dizzy, said she never should dare go back over the bridges. He asked her jokingly if he should take her back to the shore in a boat, and she replied, "Please do!"

21. She thought he was in earnest when she said it; but you can imagine in how short a time a boat would be borne over the fall from the rapids about the islands, and how quickly the lady would have changed her mind if she had seen a boat tied to a tree on the island shore. She soon got over her dizziness and fright and walked ashore without a word.

CHAPTER XII.

FROM BUFFALO TO CHICAGO.

1. A little way above Niagara Falls, where Niagara River flows from Lake Erie, is the city of Buffalo. Here is the western end of the Erie Canal, which crosses the State of New York from Albany to Buffalo. Here the steamers from the great western lakes bring grain and lumber from the country on their shores, and here are tall buildings called grain-elevators, in which great quantities of corn, wheat, and oats are stored.

2. The streets of Buffalo are broad and handsome, and in many of them shade-trees are growing. There are several parks and fine drives, so that it is not only a town important for its commerce, but also a pleasant one for residence.

3. Trade in large amount, like the trade in grain between Buffalo and the West, is called commerce. New York City has commercial dealings with foreign countries; but the commerce of a lake port, like Buffalo, is more with our own country. Commerce or trade with foreign coun-

tries is called foreign commerce, and the home trade is domestic commerce.

4. If you go down to the wharves in Buffalo, you will see people busied in many ways about the imports and exports, as we call the various things received and sent out from a country in its trade with other countries. For example, Java coffee from the island of Java, and bananas from Costa Rica, are imports in New York, just as grain and lumber are imports in Buffalo. Things sent out are exports.

5. Steamers for the West leave Buffalo very often. Let us take one bound for Chicago, and make an imaginary journey around the lakes.

6. For some distance after leaving Buffalo we can see the shores of New York; then we are a long way from that state. We stop at Erie in Northern Pennsylvania, and find that this state has nearly fifty miles of lake-coast, although it has no sea-coast. Erie has a very fine harbor, and Presque Isle, lying in front of the harbor, is one of the most beautiful of islands.

7. A man comes on board at Erie, who is from the Pennsylvania oil-regions, not far to the south.

He says he is going out to Chicago on business. He tells you that he always goes by the lakes during the summer season to enjoy the fine air. " But," he adds, " if I have to go out to Chicago during the winter, I go on the cars."

8. A boy, standing near him, says, " I suppose it is too cold in the winter on the steamer."

9. " Yes, too cold for me, and too cold for the steamer," answers the traveller. " Fresh water freezes more readily than salt water, and there are several months of the year when the Great Lakes are partly frozen over. Steamers cannot go back and forth on Lake Erie all winter, as they can on the Atlantic Ocean. Navigation closes on the Great Lakes during the coldest months.

10. " Sometimes, during a mild winter, there is very little ice in the lakes. But I have seen the time when you could drive across Lake Erie on the ice with horses and sleighs."

11. " I have heard that it is a very dangerous lake. Why is that ? " says the boy.

12. " Because it is so shallow. It is not much more than one hundred feet deep; and the winds ruffle it up, and drive the waters up on the shore.

That's the reason why such large breakwaters have been built out into the lake at the towns on the shore, to keep the water from blowing up into the lower streets during a heavy storm."

13. Lake Erie is about two hundred and forty miles long. We ride all night after leaving the Pennsylvania coast, off the coast of Ohio. In the morning we stop at Cleveland, a large city, which is one of the most beautiful of all the cities in our country. It certainly looks very lovely from the deck of our lake steamer. We can see the white houses, shining among the green trees, on the high plain overlooking the water; and through the city the river comes winding down to the lake.

14. Sandusky is another pleasant city on the Ohio coast, some distance west of Cleveland. There are a number of islands out a little way in the lake. On one of these we see a picnic fishing-party. They wave their hats and handkerchiefs to us as we sail by.

15. Toledo is another Ohio city of which we have a glimpse as we sail along. It is five miles from the shore of the lake, on Maumee Bay, a

widening of the Maumee River, which here flows
into Lake Erie.

16. Soon after losing sight of Toledo, the lake
grows narrower and narrower, and presently we
can see the other shore. Then we come into a
deep blue river, the Detroit River. The current
is swift; but our steamer makes good headway,
and soon we have reached the wharves of Detroit.

17. This is the largest city in the State of
Michigan. Lansing is the capital, but it is an
inland city; and we cannot visit it at present.
Another important place near Detroit is Ann
Arbor. The University of Michigan is at Ann
Arbor. It is one of the best universities in the
United States, and has more students, both men
and women, than any other.

18. At Detroit we see a whole train of cars,
crossing the river on a big ferry-boat. It is an
interesting sight. There are railroad tracks on
the flat top of the huge ferry-boat. The cars are
pushed upon these by an engine while the ferry-
boat is close to the shore. Then the engine in the
boat goes to work, and the train is ferried across
the river.

19. Detroit is an important commercial city, and a great deal of lumber is sold here, that comes from the forests of Northern Michigan. There are many iron manufactories here, too; and if you go through Detroit in the night, the big, bright chimneys remind you of the chimneys of Pittsburg.

20. Above Detroit, as shown on the map, and above it by the direction of the river current, too, is Lake St. Clair. This is not one of the five Great Lakes, and it looks quite small between Lake Erie and the great Lake Huron further north. But Lake St. Clair is thirty miles wide. You see it is not very tiny, although it has been called "The Baby of the Lakes," it is so much smaller than the rest.

21. A swift and broad river, the St. Clair River, connects this lake with Lake Huron. Up this river our steamer goes for nearly forty miles. We pass the town of Port Huron, and are out on blue Lake Huron. Now for more than two days and nights we sail away northward to the Straits of Mackinaw; and we are out of sight of the land night and day. We could easily believe that we were out on the great ocean itself.

22. To the west of us, all the way, is the coast of Michigan, with its bays and its towns, and as we near the straits, the great dark forests appear. There are many islands in the Straits of Mackinaw; but our pilot is a good one, and steers us safely past them all. After we pass the Beaver Islands, we turn directly to the south into Lake Michigan. And now we are sailing southward for days still out of sight of land in this inland sea.

23. Green Bay, extending into the state of Wisconsin to the west of us, is named from the deep green of the water in the bay. Its shores are favorite resorts for summer camping-parties from Wisconsin towns and from places further south.

24. On our way down the Wisconsin coast we stop at a large city, Milwaukee. It is sometimes called the "Cream City," because pretty cream-colored bricks are much used in the buildings. From the steamer we can see that it is a very clean and handsome city.

25. Racine is another Wisconsin city on the coast south of Milwaukee. Then, if we go down the Illinois coast, all the way to Chicago, we are

THE WATER WORKS TOWER.

in sight of pretty suburban towns in groves along
the shore. Sometimes high bluffs rise up from
the water. We see the light from the light-house

at Evanston, as we sail by. This is the place where a large steamer, the Lady Elgin, was lost many years ago.

26. Now we come to the mouth of the Chicago River, and see the masts of many vessels, the high grain-elevators, and the spires of churches. Out in the lake is a stone tower, which is at the end of a long tunnel under the bed of the lake. Through this tunnel water for the city's supply is pumped to the tower of the water-works, that we can see on the land.

CHAPTER XIII.

OHIO AND INDIANA.

1. We could have made the journey from Buffalo to Chicago by train in a day, instead of taking nearly a week as on the boat journey around the lakes. If we had gone by train, we should have travelled quite across two rich farming states, Ohio and Indiana.

2. Ohio was once nearly covered by groves of trees ; though there is prairie-land near the lake in the northwestern part of the state. But many

millions of these trees have been cut down and burned; and where the forests once stood are now fine farms.

3. Many sheep are raised in Ohio, and it is pleasant to see the white animals, sheep and lambs, running about over the hills. Ohio is a hilly state, and thousands of grape-vines grow on the hills; but there are no mountains in the state.

4. One of the most interesting things in Ohio is the Great Divide, a high ridge of land over two hundred miles long. This divides the country so that the rivers on the north of it flow towards Lake Erie, and those on the south towards the Ohio River.

5. This great river, you remember, starts at Pittsburgh where two smaller rivers join to form it. It is the southern boundary of Ohio, Indiana, and Illinois, and flows into the Mississippi River.

6. Cincinnati, the largest city in Ohio, is in the southern part of the state on the banks of the Ohio River. The city is built on two high terraces above the river. A gray stone, not so pretty as the cream-colored brick of Milwaukee, but of a very good color, is chiefly used for building.

7. There are many handsome public buildings. The opera-houses of Cincinnati are noted ; the people are extremely fond of music. A fine fountain with sculptured figures, and surrounded by trees, is one of the chief ornaments of Cincinnati.

8. Back of the terraces on which the main streets of the city are built, are many hills which are terraced with streets. These hills are covered with houses quite to their summits. From the piazzas may be seen steamers and other vessels far up and down the broad Ohio, loaded with wool, pork, and many other products of the west.

9. Across the river is Covington, some of whose streets are a continuation of those in Cincinnati. Covington is in the State of Kentucky, although it is only across the river. A fine suspension bridge connects this smaller city with Cincinnati. Many persons whose business is in Cincinnati have their homes in Covington.

10. The Miami Canal, which crosses Ohio from north to south, enters a basin at Cincinnati. It is cut through the Great Divide, and the northern end of the canal is at Toledo, which, as you remember, is near Lake Erie.

11. By this canal large quantities of grain, potatoes, and other produce from the farms of Ohio are carried to market. Indian corn grows in the Ohio fields. Hogs are raised in great numbers and pork-packing is an important business in Cincinnati.

12. Columbus, the capital of Ohio, is nearly in the centre of the state, on the banks of the Scioto, one of the rivers which flow into the Ohio. A good deal of manufacturing in iron is carried on in Columbus, and there is a large trade in coal. A great deal of coal is mined in this part of the state, and also in the southeastern part.

13. Look on the map and see how near you are to Pittsburgh when in Southeastern Ohio. A narrow region of country, belonging to the State of West Virginia, extends northward like the handle of a big pan, between this part of Ohio and Pennsylvania. In this "pan-handle" is the city of Wheeling, which is the capital of West Virginia. Akron, Zanesville, Springfield, and Dayton are other cities in Ohio.

14. West of Ohio is the State of Indiana. In the southern part of Indiana there are many low,

rough hills where limestone is found in abundance, from which lime is made. The farms in this part of the state are not as fertile as they are further north, though there are many rivers; and along the banks of these, except where they are marshy, there is much fine farming land, especially in the valley of the Wabash.

15. New Albany and Evansville are two cities on the Ohio River in the southern part of the state, and Terre Haute, further north, is on the Wabash River. All around this town is a rich, level farming country, where not a hill is to be seen, and where Indian corn grows in the big fields.

16. Indianapolis, the capital of the state, is the largest city in Indiana. Its streets are wide and shaded with trees. The State House is a fine building, and from the dome the outlook is over a great plain surrounding the city. There are coal mines not far away, and farms, villages, and great groves of black-walnut trees from which much beautiful furniture is made.

17. It is so warm in Indianapolis in the summer time, that it seems somewhat like a South-

ern city. There are many colored people in the place who came up from the South.

18. Michigan City is the only town in Indiana on the lake coast. The southern shore of Lake Michigan is part of the northern boundary of the state. Michigan City is more important, however, as a railroad town than as a lake port.

19. For many miles west of Michigan City, along the shores of the lake, are immense sand dunes, or hills, made of shifting sand. Nothing grows on these dunes, and the sands are constantly blown about by winds from the lake.

20. Sometimes fishing parties from some inland village go to the lake by way of these hills, finding their way through the little valleys where stunted evergreens grow. To come out upon the broad, beautiful sandy beach of the blue lake, after walking through the sand-hills, is a pleasant experience.

21. People often come from Chicago to Michigan City on small lake steamers, to enjoy the sail on the lake; they can easily go and come in a day on a lake steamer, and on the train the journey is made more quickly.

CHAPTER XIV.

IN CHICAGO.

1. Coming into Chicago on the train from Indiana, you pass through a great number of small towns and villages, scattered about over the prairie-land, which surrounds the great city   In many places you see miles of broad sidewalks, built beside streets which seem like country roads. You wonder at this; but if you look, you will see everywhere on the land, near these board side-walks, signs, saying that lots are for sale. This accounts for it.

2. The ground in many places about Chicago is low and marshy; and although it is drained and made into pleasant sites for houses as fast as these suburban places are built up, still the first thing that is necessary to get people to think of living in the newer suburbs, is to give them sidewalks to walk upon.

3. These new places are built up rapidly, for Chicago grows very fast; and the people must

have homes in the suburbs, because there is not room in the city for them all.

4. As you near the city, you see the smoking chimneys of a great manufactory in a large town on the lake shore, called South Chicago. Steel rails for railroads are made at South Chicago. It is very interesting to see how the steel is made of melted iron that comes out of the furnace like running brooks of fire, and is afterwards moulded into rails on great machines. When the rails have cooled and hardened they are ready to be laid on the wooden ties of a railroad bed.

5. There are a great number of railroads coming into Chicago from every direction. One way of entering the city is along the shore of the lake. The railroad tracks are very near the water's edge. From the car windows, as you ride into the city over these tracks, you can see the waves of the lake dashing up against long breakwaters, which, not unlike piers, are built out from the shore. There are frequently men and boys to be seen fishing on these breakwaters.

6. As your train comes down into the city, you pass a large, open, grassy place, planted with a few

trees. Across this park, on Michigan Avenue, you can see a very large and handsome new building. It is called the Auditorium, and has an immense hall capable of holding many thousands of people.

7. President Harrison was the first President nominated in the Auditorium, which was not completed at the time he was nominated. Before this building was made, the national conventions had been held for a number of years in the Exposition Building, an older and far less beautiful building, a little way down Michigan Avenue. Your train goes directly behind this building, which is very near the lake shore.

8. A few streets below, you step from the train, and go out into the streets of Chicago. In this part of the city are the high buildings used for the wholesale trade. Not far from the station, and near the place where the Chicago River flows into the lake, is a wholesale grocery house, which has a marble tablet set in the wall, saying that here stood the old log building, Fort Dearborn. This fort was the first building erected where this great city now stands.

9. Thousands of people now living remember

when Chicago was a little village, and Indians and trappers were the only people who traded with those who kept the small shops in the place. In those days all the country round about was wild and uncultivated. But the land is rich and fertile in Illinois, and, indeed, all about Chicago for hundreds of miles; and people soon found that they could make homes for themselves quickly in this part of the country.

10. Great lines of railway were built; farms were made on the new prairie-land; wheat, corn, and oats were raised in enormous quantities; and the village soon grew to be a large city.

11. Probably more wheat is bought and sold in Chicago now than in any other city in the world. All visitors to Chicago go to see the new Board of Trade building.

12. You may take a walk through the broad streets, when you have looked as long as you like at that marble tablet on the store which stands on the site of old Fort Dearborn. The streets cross each other at right angles.

13. There are no irregular or narrow streets in Chicago, and no hills. It is built on perfectly flat

ground, and some of the longer streets extend for miles without a rise of ground or a turning of any sort.

14. You cross Michigan Avenue on your way up from the station. In this part of the street are business buildings and hotels; but a half mile southward, the fine houses begin, which extend for several miles in this direction.

15. Very many of these houses are in the modern styles of beautiful architecture. A pale, gray-green stone, which comes from the Lake Superior country, is used for a few fine houses. This makes an artistic contrast with the dark red brick and the stone of other colors used for most of the houses.

16. As you go through the streets "down town" in Chicago, you notice that everybody seems to be in a hurry. You must use even greater care in crossing the streets than you found necessary in New York. Most of the street-cars here are run by a cable laid under the streets, and connecting with great engines in different parts of the city. These cable-cars go very fast.

17. If you get into a car of one of these trains,

you can ride out to South Park. Here you will find pleasant park-wagons, as in Central Park, and broad drives called boulevards.

18. Along Drexel Boulevard are beautiful beds of bright flowers, and in the park is a large conservatory, where you may see flowers of all kinds, to your heart's content. When it is too cold for them to grow out-of-doors, — and it is often bitterly cold in Chicago in the winter, — the flowers of the boulevards find shelter in the conservatory.

19. There are a number of fine parks about Chicago, and boulevards lead from one to another; so that you might have a drive of thirty-five miles from park to park around this great city.

20. When you have returned to the business part of the city from your ride to South Park, you can get into another cable-car and go through the tunnel under the river to the North Side, and out to Lincoln Park.

21. The bridges over the Chicago River are made to turn, to allow lake-steamers to come up stream to the grain-elevators. If you are in a hurry to cross the river, and the drawbridge is turned for a steamer, it is not agreeable to wait

for it to turn back, and the tunnels under the stream make it possible for people to go more quickly.

22. On the way to Lincoln Park you will see pleasant streets and many handsome houses and churches, and you will pass stores and shops without number in the business streets through which you go. In Lincoln Park is a very noble statue of President Lincoln, made by a famous sculptor, Augustus St. Gaudens.

23. You have now been out upon the North Side and the South Side of the city. A third portion, called the West Side, lies across the river in another direction.

24. Many visitors to Chicago go to see the stock-yards, where are cattle, sheep, and hogs by thousands, brought in cars from the stock-farms of the great West to be made into beef, mutton, and pork.

25. The cars for carrying live-stock are made with spaces between the boards to enable the animals to breathe while coming to the great slaughter-houses. The meat is sent to the Eastern cities. Large quantities of it are canned and sent to England and Russia, and other distant countries.

26. A boy who had always lived on a great stock-farm in Illinois, was taken to the city for his first visit. His father asked him if he would not like to go out to the stock-yards. The boy knew that his father had just sent a train of twenty cars of stock to the yards, and his answer was; "No, papa. I'm afraid I might see them killing some poor cow that I am acquainted with."

27. There are many manufactories in and near Chicago. The coal used is chiefly a soft coal which makes a very thick smoke. The wind blows most of the time, otherwise the dust and soot would be most unpleasant.

CHAPTER XV.

ILLINOIS PRAIRIES.

1. Illinois is a prairie state. When it was admitted into the Union, much of it was an unfenced plain. Now it is covered with railroads, towns, cities, and farms. The wild flowers that grew in profusion on the uncultivated lands have given place to fields of Indian corn, oats, wheat,

and buckwheat, and to meadows of timothy grown for hay. Eighty acres are often fenced in for one hay-field.

2. When the wind blows across a big timothy meadow, just before the hay is ready for cutting, the grasses, swaying as the wind bends them, look like waves of the lake. If the sky is clouded here and there, and both shadows and sunshine fall upon the field, the bowing of the grasses seems even more like the light and dark of the waves, as they rise and fall.

3. Although old-fashioned fences of rails and boards, and new-fashioned fences of cruel barbed wire are much used in Illinois, a favorite way of dividing the fields is by hedges of osage orange.

4. This is common in other Western states also. It is a thorny hedge, and the leaves are long and glossy. The fruit is green in color and not good to eat, but it makes fine balls to play with. These hedges grow as high as cherry trees, if not trimmed down, and give the treeless prairies a pleasant look.

5. Within thirty miles of Chicago, to the south-west, are prairies where for many miles there is

not a tree that has not been planted. Along the creeks there are natural groves of trees,—hickories, black-walnuts, butternuts, oaks and maples.

6. Lombardy poplars—tall, straight trees—are planted on almost every farm in this part of the country. Driving across the prairies, you can tell the location of any distant farm-house by the group of trees planted about it, and especially by the poplars standing up high like church steeples above the roofs.

7. The water in the creeks on the prairies does not run so fast as the brooks of Eastern states, where the country is hilly. There is so little slope to the land of the prairies that the water in these prairie creeks moves very slowly.

8. Slough grasses and flowers grow quite to their edges, and the ground is so dark and rich that the blue-flags and other flowers are often reflected in water which appears to be brown. But if you take up a little water in your hand, you find it as clear as if it were flowing down fast over a rocky bed, instead of creeping along over a loamy one lined with thick grasses.

9. The Indian corn in the great fields of the

West is usually planted with rows both ways, like a checker-board. The corn-planting machines are made so that the kernels are dropped into the ground at even distances. Then when the corn grows up, and tassels out, each stalk is exactly the same distance from its nearest neighbor.

10. It is delightful to drive along a prairie road on a summer day, during the time of the harvest of oats, and see the great fields of yellow grain with the reapers at work. There is the wide yellow track round the field where the machine has cut the grain, and the oats still standing in the centre of the field. There are the bundles which have been tied up and lie drying and ripening in the sun. The sky is blue, and the green osage hedge shines in rich contrast with the ripe grain.

11. You may travel all over the State of Illinois, and see thousands of such scenes. Everywhere railroads cross the farms and fields, and everywhere are pleasant towns; while white schoolhouses dot the country, as stars dot the sky.

12. The Chicago River, which used to be a narrow, sloughy stream, has been widened and

deepened for the entrance of lake steamers. It is one of the few rivers in Illinois which flow into Lake Michigan. Most of the others, large and small, find their way into the Mississippi River, which is the western boundary line of the state.

13. The creeks of Illinois flow into the little rivers, and the little rivers into the large ones, — the Illinois River, Rock River, and the Kaskaskia River, — and these all empty into the Mississippi.

14. In the southeastern part of the state some of the streams flow towards the Wabash River, which for a long distance separates Illinois from Indiana. The Wabash flows south into the Ohio River. But this, as you remember, flows into the Mississippi, in its turn.

15. At the mouth of the Ohio River, where it empties into the Mississippi, is the town of Cairo. North of Cairo is a large coal region. At the town of Peoria, much further north, the Illinois River widens into a pretty lake called Peoria Lake. There are high bluffs on the Illinois River at Peoria. Joliet, famous for its stone quarries, Aurora, Bloomington, and Elgin, where the Elgin watches are made, are other cities of Illinois.

16. In the central part of the state, not far from the river Sangamon, is Springfield, the capital of Illinois. Here was the home of President Lincoln.

17. It was from the steps of the train on which he went away to Washington to become President of the United States that Mr. Lincoln said good by to his old friends and neighbors. You know that he never returned, living, to his old home. His grave is at Springfield.

18. "Not for thy sheaves nor savannas
    Crown we thee, proud Illinois!
    Here in his grave is thy grandeur;
    Born of his sorrow thy joy.

19. "Over our Washington's river
    Sunrise beams rosy and fair,
    Sunset on Sangamon fairer,
    Father and martyr lies there.

20. "Sangamon, stream of the prairies!
    Placidly westward that flows,
    Far in whose city of silence,
    Calm he has sought his repose."

CHAPTER XVI.

KENTUCKY AND THE MAMMOTH CAVE.

1. South of the States of Illinois, Indiana, and Ohio is Kentucky. You remember that the suspension bridge over the Ohio River at Cincinnati connects that city with Covington, which is in Kentucky.

2. Kentucky is a very long state from east to west; but as the distance from the river on the north to the southern boundary line is not very great, it is, after all, not much larger than Indiana, the smallest of the three states north of it. The rivers in Kentucky flow towards the Ohio River; so you see, that you are still in the basin of the Mississippi while in Kentucky.

3. In the eastern part of Kentucky are the Cumberland Mountains. These are part of the Appalachian system, the same system to which the Green Mountains of Vermont and the Blue Ridge of Pennsylvania belong.

4. They all form the great divide which sepa-

rates the rivers of the great lakes and the Mississippi valley from those of the Atlantic slope. The
scenery of the Cumberland Mountains is very picturesque, and several large rivers have their rise
in the springs of the Cumberland.

5. All the way from the Big Sandy River westward to the Cumberland River, covering more
than half of the state, is a famous tract of land
called The Blue Grass Country. It is a hilly
country, and the limestone which abounds here is
of a bluish tint.

6. Kentucky blue-grass is as green as any other
grass; but it grows plentifully on these blue hills,
and forms a fine pasture for the horses for which
this region is celebrated. Kentucky horses bring
good prices everywhere, and they are raised in
great numbers.

7. Imagine yourself standing by the fence of a
great pasture where five hundred horses are feeding.
One inquiring colt comes towards you. Perhaps
he puts his nose through the bars of the fence.
Another colt joins him; then come their mothers,
and three or four yearlings, the colts of last year.

8. Soon twenty others join them to see what

they are interested in. Before you know it. a hundred of the beautiful slender-limbed animals, of differing ages, most of them bay in color and sleek of coat, are looking at you from the other side of the fence.

9. Something startles them. Perhaps you climb up on the fence, and they think you are going to catch some of them: They love their freedom; and before you can think, they turn and go galloping off like the wind over the breezy knolls of the broad pasture.

10. Hemp and tobacco, both plants that need a mild Southern climate, grow in Kentucky. A field of hemp in blossom is a beautiful sight. When you think that the ropes made from Kentucky hemp are used all over the country, you will remember this blossoming field.

11. Louisville is the largest city in Kentucky, and Frankfort is the capital of the state.

12. Louisville is on the banks of the Ohio River. The river here is very rapid; people speak of "the falls" at Louisville; although when the river is high, steamboats go up and down the rapids instead of through the canal.

13. The gardens and lawns about the houses of this city are generally large and pleasant ones, and flowers grow out of doors much later in the autumn than in more northerly places.

14. Pork-packing is a good business in Louisville, as well as the shipping of tobacco, hemp, and other productions of the state, and the sugar-curing of hams is carried on by many firms.

15. Near the Green River in the western part of Kentucky is one of the largest caves in the world. It is called the Mammoth Cave. Mammoth means very large, — enormous.

16. You could not possibly walk about everywhere in this great cavern. If we visit it, you must content yourself with only a peep at its wonderful rooms and grottos. Not even the people who own it, and whom we pay to show us a little of the cave, have seen all of its nooks and corners.

17. The cave reaches nine miles under the ground, and to explore all of the rooms and galleries branching from the main one would take nearly two hundred miles of travel.

18. If you are to visit the cave, put on flannel

suits like gymnasium suits, instead of your usual
clothes, and over these wear oil-cloth suits
like those you put on to go under the falls at
Niagara. This is to keep off the water
which drips from the roof of some parts of the
cave. Then, following your guides who carry
lights, go down into the cave.

19. In this dark underground world, you see,
as you walk on, wonderful rooms, one after another, arched with white stones in all sorts of
strange and beautiful forms, that glitter as
the light falls upon them.

20. Down from the roofs hang long shining
stalactites, that look like great white icicles. The
water, slowly dripping through from the earth
above, has made the stone roof of the cave take
all sorts of fantastic and flowery shapes.

21. All around you are pillars and posts of the
stone, shining in the light of your guides' torches.
Some of these pillars reach to the roof; others
are only a few feet high. In these avenues which
are not much higher than ordinary rooms, the
white walls do not seem so wonderful as when you
come out into one of the great rooms, like the

Star Chamber. Here you can scarcely see the roof.

22. Your guides conduct you up ladders and over streams of water. You stand near the edge of one of the deep pits, — the Maelstrom or the Bottomless Pit, — and toss in pebbles, which you hear rattling away, down, down, till at last the sound ceases, and you cannot guess how deep nor how far they have gone.

23. At Echo River you toss pebbles again, this time into a stream running where the sun never shines upon it. Fishes without eyes have been found in Echo River. Over the river Styx you cross on a natural bridge formed of stone which arches the deep black water. When the guide tells you that fishes with eyes have been taken from the river Styx, you ask, "Of what good are their eyes to them, since they live here in this sunless cavern?"

24. "None," he answers; "for they are all blind. Nature does not bother them with sight when they will never need it. But, as strange as it may seem to you, they can swim just as well in the dark."

CHAPTER XVII.

VIRGINIA AND THE CAROLINAS.

1. If we go over the Cumberland Mountains eastward from Kentucky, we find ourselves in the State of Virginia. We are in a picturesque mountainous country. As we travel northward through the valleys of the Blue Ridge, we find small towns and pretty farms. We come to the Peaks of Otter. From these high mountains we can look out over the tobacco fields and farms round about the city of Lynchburg.

2. In the spring when the tobacco plant is in blossom, you would not imagine what it could be, if you had never before seen it growing. But when it is ripe, and hangs dry upon the stalks, it would not be so hard to recognize it. All the way to Richmond, the capital, we may see large fields of tobacco, and great quantities of it are shipped from that city.

3. Going northward, and on our mountain journey, we shall not see much tobacco growing, but more grains and fruits. All through these

Virginia mountains there are mineral springs of various sorts. We must see the White Sulphur Springs in West Virginia.

4. Like Saratoga in the North, this town is a favorite resort for people who do not care to take the waters for their health, as well as for those who do. It is a pleasant place to visit for any reason. We see groups of people dressed in white, sitting upon the hotel piazzas in the pleasant summer evening, or walking about under the trees.

5. Down the beautiful Shenandoah valley we go northward until we reach the Potomac River at the town of Harper's Ferry. Here both the Shenandoah and the Potomac force their way through the mountains, and all around us we see the most romantic and delightful scenes.

6. We passed Harper's Ferry on our first boat journey up the Potomac, although we were then making acquaintance with the river, rather than with the towns along its banks. The Potomac is the northern boundary of Virginia, and we may now repeat for a little distance our first journey down the river.

7. We will go in a steamboat instead of a row-boat, and stop at Alexandria on the Virginia shore. We can see the dome of the Capitol across the river at Washington, and we learn now that the home and tomb of General Washington that we visited are in Virginia too.

8. Richmond, the capital and the largest city of the state, is a hundred miles south of Mount Vernon, on the banks of the James River. We see the smoking chimneys of many manufactories in our walks about this pleasant city on the hills.

9. The falls of the James River make the working power for the machinery of the mills and manufactories. In the Capitol park we come upon a statue of General Washington, — a famous statue by the sculptor Houdon.

10. A little more than a hundred miles west of Richmond is the celebrated Natural Bridge. It is worth going a long way to see. Adar Creek, a shallow stream, has worn its way through the rocks of a deep chasm. At one end of this chasm the rock joins, high above the creek, in an arch.

11. Nature has made a bridge of stone over this little stream, and people walk and drive across it on

the pub-
lic road.
Think
of riding over a
fine, stone, arched
bridge, which no
man ever worked
to build!

12. The journey
down to Fortress
Monroe and Old

THE NATURAL BRIDGE

Point Comfort from Richmond gives us glimpses of a different sort of country. For after we have passed the plantations, or farms, our train takes us through great forests of yellow pine, oak, cypress, and locust.

13. Norfolk must be visited. Here thousands of boxes of strawberries are shipped in early spring to Northern cities. Early vegetables are sent to New York and Boston, too, long before it is time for them to be ripe in the market gardens near these cities.

14. South of Norfolk, and extending southward for forty miles, into North Carolina, is a great morass called the Dismal Swamp. It is not so dismal a region as its name seems to show ; for there is a canal made through the marsh, and it furnishes a great deal of timber for use in making ships and railroad ties, and also for making shingles. There is something very cheerful in the sight of a load of clean shingles, being carried far away to make roofs for houses, stables, and schoolhouses.

15. Two large sounds extend into the land of North Carolina. They are separated from the Atlantic Ocean by long and narrow islands. Be-

tween these islands are numerous straits leading into the sounds, which are called Albemarle Sound and Pamlico Sound.

16. The waters here are usually smooth, for they are sheltered from the rough winds of the Atlantic. Coasting vessels, trading between Norfolk and Newbern, pass through these sounds. But steamers from the South, sailing in the open Atlantic outside these sheltering islands, usually pass by them a good way out at sea.

17. Look on the map, and you will see how the land of one of these islands juts out into the sea at Cape Hatteras. It is a stormy coast, and sailors expect gales while " off Hatteras."

18. Wilmington, near the coast, at the mouth of Cape Fear River, is the largest city in North Carolina. A great deal of turpentine, rosin, tar, and pitch, as well as cotton, are shipped from Wilmington.

19. Raleigh, the capital of North Carolina, is near the central part of the state. In all the capitals you may visit, you will find few State Houses more beautiful than the one at Raleigh. It is of granite, and from its outlook you can see

the pretty city on the hill and the cotton plantations round about.

20. In the western part of North Carolina are the Black Mountains. Here the peaks are as high as those of the White Mountains in New Hampshire; and Mount Mitchell is higher than Mount Washington, the highest of the White Mountains. Both of them are more than a mile high.

21. There are a number of mountains a mile high near Mount Mitchell in North Carolina, but this is the last group of high mountains that we see in going southward. This is the southern group of the Appalachian system; the White Mountains form the most northern one, hundreds of miles away.

22. We have been in a cotton-growing country in North Carolina. In South Carolina, we find ourselves further still into " the land of the cotton and the cane." Sugar-cane, from which sugar and molasses are made, grows on almost all of the upland farms of South Carolina.

23. Sugar-cane looks very much like Indian corn, while growing in the field. The stalks

grow about as high, and have long, green, banner-like leaves. But there are no ears of corn on the sugar-cane; and the leaves are all stripped from the sweet and juicy stalks before they go into the mill that presses out the thick sweet liquid from which sugar is made.

24. You must see the rice-fields on the low 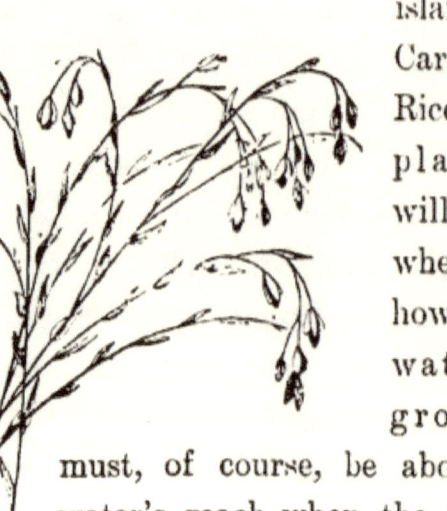 islands of the Carolina coast. Rice is a thirsty plant, as you will easily guess when you see how much it is watered while growing. It must, of course, be above the salt water's reach when the tide is high. But on the islands that are sometimes overflowed rice grows well.

RICE PLANT.   And on many of the plantations, ditches with gates are arranged, so that the fields may be flooded when the farmers think it necessary.

25. It is pleasant to stand on the piazza of a plantation home, and look across the fields where the green plant is growing, and think how, by and by, the seeds of this plant will be made into puddings, or served with cream for boys and girls thousands of miles away.

26. The rice-bird likes the seeds too; and all sorts of devices are invented to frighten him away. He is

A RICE FIELD.

a dainty morsel himself when broiled, and has more to fear from hunters' guns than from scarecrows.

27. The rice-bird spends his summers in the North, where he is called the bobolink. Everybody admires the music of his song, and nobody

ever reminds him that he is a great annoyance to the Carolina rice-growers when he is at home.

28. Rice and cotton are both shipped in enormous quantities from Charleston, the largest city in South Carolina.

CHAPTER XVIII.

IN THE SOUTH.

1. Savannah is one of the largest cities in Georgia. This state is separated from South Carolina by the Savannah River. The city of Savannah is about eighteen miles from the mouth of the river. Steamers come up the broad Savannah from the ocean, and are loaded with cotton and rice for distant ports.

2. Come to the river, down from the streets of the city shaded by live oaks, to the wharves below the high bluffs along the river front. Here you see the huge bales of cotton, as they are brought down and loaded upon the steamers, which are to carry them away to the manufactories.

3. After watching the people at work here

for a time, you may go up into the city again, past the rice warehouses, and on into the quiet streets, where the tulip laurel grows, and where flowers bloom in the gardens from March until New Year's.

4. It is warmer here in winter than in any place we have yet visited. There are many boys and girls in Georgia who have no idea of the pleasures of coasting and skating, just as there are many boys and girls in the North who cannot imagine themselves picking roses out of doors at Christmas time.

5. River steamers go up the Savannah to the pleasant city of Augusta. On the way you can see, from your place on the deck, distant fields of cotton. The cotton is planted in rows; and in the springtime, the colored people, who do much of the work in the Southern fields, are busy hoeing out the weeds, which would otherwise grow faster than the cotton in the warm sunshine.

6. In the summer, when the cotton is ready for picking, you will see the white fields full of dark people, picking off the cotton, as it bursts open in a fluffy ball on top of the plant. It goes on ripen-

ing and opening for several months. You know, in popping corn, some kernels pop out white in the heat of the fire sooner than others; and it

A COTTON FIELD.

is the same with the balls of cotton in the heat of the Southern sun.

7. The cotton is picked, and carried in bags to the cotton-gin. This is a machine which separates the seeds from the fibre of the cotton. Then the cotton is pressed into big bundles, called bales; and you have seen how these are loaded upon steamers at the

ports, and carried away to be made into ginghams, prints, sheetings, and fine muslins. There are now many cotton mills in the Southern States as well as in the North.

8. The most delicate and beautiful cotton fabrics are made from sea-island cotton, which grows on the low islands along the coast. This cotton has a very fine fibre, and it is from sea-island cotton that the best threads are made.

9. From Augusta to Atlanta, the capital of Georgia, is a pleasant ride by train. You can see the city of Atlanta at a distance, for it is on higher ground than the surrounding country. A number of railroads pass through Atlanta. One of these runs through the central part of the state.

10. You can go north on this railroad through the mountains, where iron and copper are found, to Chattanooga, just over the border in the State of Tennessee. On your way you will see a great many fruit trees and large fields of potatoes and corn, but not much cotton. Or you may go south through the cotton and tobacco fields of central Georgia to the sea.

11. The Georgia sea-islands have a great many palmetto trees growing on them. The palmetto grows in Florida, also, and there are many other trees which grow wild here that could not live in the cold Northern climate.

12. Cypress and magnolia, mahogany, the dogwood with its fragrant blossoms and live oaks hung with long gray mosses, are among the trees. Orange trees are cultivated in Florida, as you already know. Some of the largest and sweetest of the Florida oranges grow in the Indian River country.

13. In the streets of Jacksonville, the largest city in the state, a great many orange trees of a variety with very sour fruit grow as ornamental trees. Visitors in the city — and Jacksonville is a city of hotels, filled with visitors during many months of the year — often express surprise that the oranges are not picked from these trees. But a taste of the fruit makes any one understand why the boys in the street leave them hanging where they are. In the groves near the city delicious oranges grow.

14. Strawberries and other fruits and early vegetables are sent north from Jacksonville. Steamers come up the St. John's River from the Atlantic Ocean, bringing dry-goods, dishes, and other articles of Northern manufacture, and carrying away the products of Florida.

15. St. Augustine. on the Atlantic coast, is the oldest town in the United States. In it there is an old fort. built by the Spaniards long, long ago. and there are ruins of an old Spanish wall which was built for the defence of the city.

16. Florida is a great peninsula, and the southern part of the state is nearly all one vast swamp. with streams and lagoons connecting Lake Okeechobee with the sea.

17. Look on the map and you will see just how this land comes out into the ocean ; and you will see the group of small islands lying south of the peninsula. Key West is the largest one of these islands: it was made by the coral insect, and is now grown over with a shrub called chaparral.

CHAPTER XIX.

THE GULF STATES.

1. If you were at Key West. and should go northward in a coasting steamer, you would be for several days on the waters of the Gulf of Mexico. You would pass the pleasant town of

Cedar Keys, on the west coast of Florida, at the mouth of the Suwanee River, which is associated everywhere by the old song, " Way down upon the Swanee River," with the thought of home.

2. In the Appalachee Bay you would not be very far from Tallahassee, the capital of Florida. This is one of the very few capital cities in our country which is not on a river or on the coast. The railroad from Tallahassee comes down to the coast of Appalachee Bay.

3. West of the capital is a part of Florida which is not a part of the great peninsula. Your steamer is now south of the land, in following the coast, instead of west of the land, as when you were coming up past Cedar Keys.

4. There are a great many low sandy islands along this coast, and the water of the bay reaches into lakes called bayous, where the water is brackish. You see many alligators in these bayous; but the negro children, playing on the shores in the sunshine, do not seem to be as much afraid of them as you would be, if you were in their places. It is very warm here all the year round. Indeed the water of the great Gulf

is a good deal warmer than it is out in the ocean itself.

5. There is a current which flows out of the Gulf of Mexico northeast into the Atlantic Ocean, called the Gulf Stream, whose waters are warmer than the ocean; and sea-moss and weeds of the Gulf are found on it, thousands of miles away.

6. Pensacola, on Pensacola Bay, is the most western city in Florida. Soon after leaving Pensacola Bay, your steamer enters Mobile Bay from the Gulf. Mobile, the largest city in Alabama, is at the head of Mobile Bay. You are no longer on the Florida coast, you see. Alabama has little sea-coast besides this beautiful bay, on whose shores the magnolia trees bloom.

7. The Alabama River and the Tombigbee River, two great streams flowing down to form the Mobile River, rise in the low mountains of Northern Alabama. These mountains are the end of the Appalachian chain that we have seen so often.

8. Montgomery, the capital of the state, is on the Alabama River. Cotton grows everywhere in the country about the capital, and many thousands of bales are shipped from here.

9. West of Alabama is Mississippi, another of the cotton states, bordering on the Gulf of Mexico. It is a state without mountains, and without any very large cities. In our journey up the Mississippi River, we shall find that some of the towns in this state are interesting, if not very large.

10. Louisiana is the fourth Gulf state, and Texas is the fifth. They are called the Gulf states because their sea-coast is all on the Gulf of Mexico. If your coasting steamer had reached the mouth of the Mississippi River coming from Key West, you would not yet have skirted half of your country's Gulf coast. Louisiana has many hundred miles of coast; so has Texas, which is the largest of all the states. Do you remember which one is the smallest?

11. All along the coast of Louisiana and of Texas are seen low sandy islands. In the Gulf, not far from New Orleans, one of these islands was once swept over by a terrible storm.

12. It was an island which people visited as a pleasure resort, and when the storm and the sea swept over the island, there was a party in one of the hotels, and many of them were drowned as the

water rushed up over the low island into the houses.

13. Galveston, on the coast of Texas, has one of the most beautiful beaches in the world, wide and sandy; the water is warm enough for bathing at any season of the year. The city is built on an island, and has wide streets. When your steamer reaches this port, you will find yourself quite ready, after your long ride, to go ashore, walk about under the trees, and see the fine flower-gardens of the city.

14. Cotton bales are plentiful on the wharf, as in the other Southern cities we have visited. We see cattle driven upon steamers here to be carried away to England to be made into beef for our English cousins.

CHAPTER XX.

A TEXAS RANCH.

1. You have read in the last chapter that Texas is the largest state in the Union. Not many people have an idea of the size of Texas, in comparison with the other states.

2. Sometimes, to cultivate the power of observing, teachers ask their pupils which they think is longer, a horse's head or a common flour barrel. It is worth finding out, if you do not know. And it would be interesting to ask some people which they think is larger, Texas or New England.

3. "Possibly Texas is larger," some one may answer you. Indeed it is. Texas is more than four times as large as New England. There are, you remember, six states in New England. If you could put these six states into Texas, and then take all four of the neighboring Gulf states, — Florida, Alabama, Mississippi, and Louisiana, — and put them into Texas, too, there would still be room enough around the corners to build all of the large cities we have visited.

4. Most of the rivers in this vast state flow into the Gulf of Mexico; there is one very broad and important river, the Rio Grande, which separates Texas from Mexico, the country south of our own.

5. Near the coast a great deal of cotton is grown, but there is another business which occupies the farmers of inland Texas. This is the

raising of cattle and sheep for distant markets. You know that at Chicago you saw long trains loaded with live animals. Many of these animals came from the ranches or great farms of Texas.

6. Sometimes the people who own the ranches live in the cities, and hire an overseer to live on the ranches. It is the business of the overseer to attend to the owner's interests in every way. Mexicans are often employed by them to do the work on the ranch, in taking care of the cattle.

7. Frank Cary, a Northern boy, once went to visit his cousin John Cary, who lived in San Antonio. John's father had a ranch about a hundred miles from the pleasant sunny city.

8. One morning he told the boys that he was going to the ranch next day to see the cattle, and they might, if they liked, go with him. Of course they were glad to go and were up very early next morning.

9. After riding from sunrise until noon in the cars, they stopped at a little country station where they found the overseer waiting for them with a spring wagon. Away they went over the rolling prairie lands for seven miles, across the ranch of

one of their friends, until they came to the Cary Ranch.   Here they found a group of small houses of pine and of adobe, in which the people lived.

10. They were very hungry after their long ride, and glad to find dinner ready for them in the overseer's house,—a good dinner of broiled venison and of sweet potatoes larger and sweeter than any Frank had ever seen.

11. After dinner the boys went out to watch some of the men "breaking" a Texas mustang. The wild little horse did not like the saddle and bridle which were put on him, and jumped about so much that no one could mount him for a long time.   At last one of the men jumped upon the horse's back and rode off down the pasture as fast as the wild little animal could run.

12. It seemed at first as if the mustang would run upon the barbs of the wire fence that surrounded the great pasture.   But the colts learn the danger of the barbs while very young, and the mustang turned away and fell into a steady gallop, as he neared the fence.

13. "When the ranch was first fenced," said John's father, "the animals often hurt themselves on the

barbs, but it seldom happens now. At first, too, we had a good deal of trouble because people on other ranges would come and cut the wires of our fence to let their cattle come down to drink at the creek. But that sort of lawlessness is now a thing of the past in Texas. Many of the ranches are fenced now, although there are still millions of acres unfenced."

14. Frank and John were up early next day, to follow the salting wagon. Each one rode a mustang pony, which was gentler than the animal they had seen mounted for the first time the day before.

15. John's father was in the spring wagon with the overseer, who ladled out salt for the cattle from a great tub in the back of the wagon. This the cattle ate eagerly from the dewy grass, and hundreds of them came running across the pasture at sight of the wagon, to get a taste of the salt.

16. After watching the cattle for awhile, Frank and John rode away for a gallop around the fence. It was a ride of seventeen miles, following the wire fence around the pasture, and they were

tired enough to be ready for dinner on their return.

17. Mr. Cary returned to San Antonio that day, but the boys begged to stay; so they were left at the ranch for a week. It was a week full of interest to the Northern boy.

18. He killed the first rattlesnake he had ever seen. He watched the antics of the queer little praying mantis, and saw several tarantulas. He tore his clothes on the thorny bushes by the creek, and rode the wild mustang without being thrown.

19. It was the most exciting moment of his life, when he saw one of the men shoot a deer on a wooded plain twenty miles distant from the ranch-house, where they rode one day after game.

20. On another day, they visited a neighbor's sheep-ranch, and saw a flock of a thousand sheep feeding on the prairie grass. At the end of the week they returned to town, but Frank said he liked staying at the ranch much better than staying in San Antonio.

21. The parks in the Texan cities are called

plazas. This word, like ranch, the word for farm, comes from the Spanish language, which is spoken by the Mexican people. Texas once belonged to Mexico instead of to our country.

Austin is the capital of the state.

CHAPTER XXI.

NEW ORLEANS.

1. One of the most interesting cities in our country is built on land so low that great banks, called levees, are made almost all around, to keep out the waters of the river, which nearly surrounds it. This is the Mississippi River.

2. In New Orleans we are only about one hundred miles from the mouth of this great river. It is a river of many twistings and windings, and we find that here it has made a big bend in shape like a crescent, or new moon, so that the land on which the city is built follows the line of the crescent. New Orleans is often called the Crescent City.

3. One of the first things you wish to see in

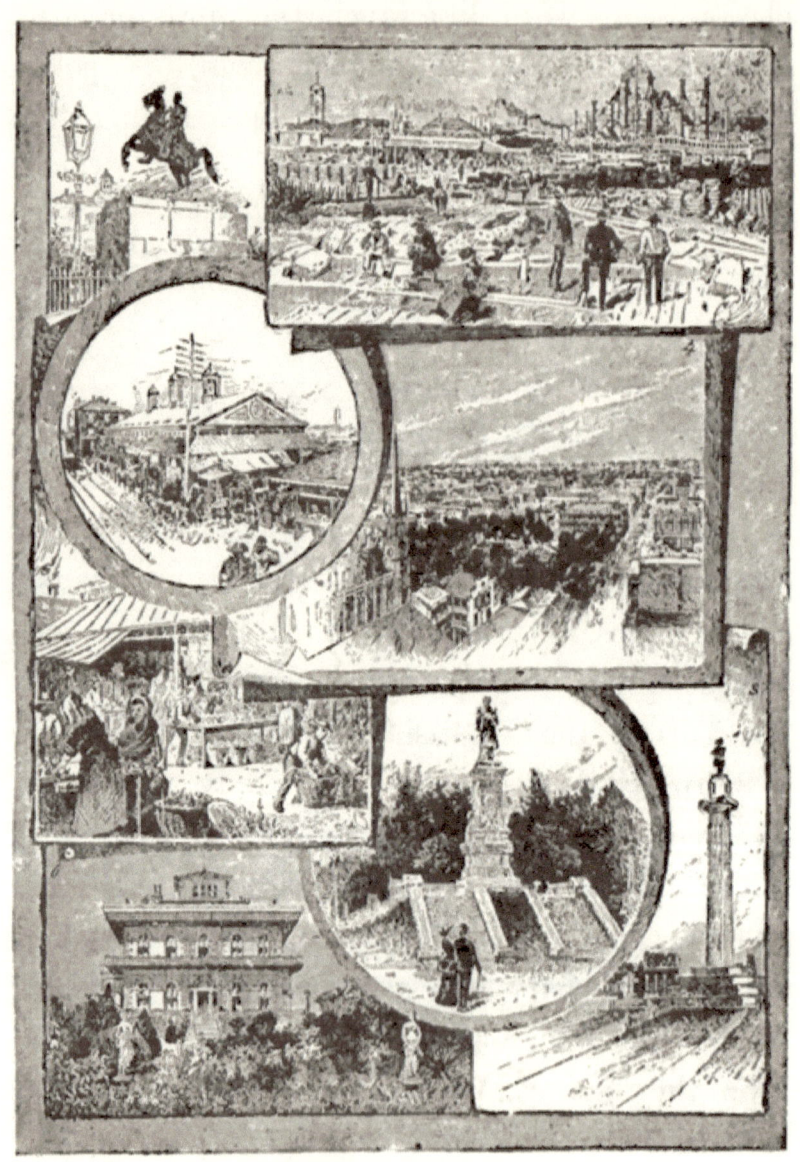

GLIMPSES OF NEW ORLEANS.

New Orleans is the way the city is protected from the great broad river. Most cities built on river banks are on land much higher than the stream, often on bluffs and hills, as at Cincinnati, or Savannah.

4. But New Orleans has grown into a large city on this low land, because it was necessary that there should be a city near the mouth of the Mississippi, and there was no high land for the city's site.

5. Standing on top of the high bank along the river, you can see why it was built, and why it is necessary to keep the levee strong and firm. Sometimes there is a rise of water in the river during spring freshets, and the city is overflowed. It would be much worse were it not for the levees. Far away to the southeast, you can see the river, as it goes on towards the Gulf of Mexico.

6. Such quantities of earth are brought down by the river that it used to be very difficult at times for steamers to get over the bar formed by the sediment at the place where the river flows into the Gulf. Often the water would be too shallow on the bar for large steamers to enter.

7. But pier-like projections, called jetties, have been built at the south entrance of the Mississippi, in a way to keep it from filling up. There are two entrances to the Mississippi. The land between is called a delta.

8. Of course you cannot see the delta from your place on the levee at New Orleans, but you can imagine how the great river finds its way on to the salt water.

9. There are always fine ocean steamers and sailing vessels to be seen from the levee, for New Orleans has a great deal of commerce with foreign countries. Enormous quantities of cotton from all the surrounding states are sent away on the ships which you see going down towards the Gulf. Others are loaded with sugar, molasses, corn, and tobacco.

10. You may be certain that the water-casks of all these sea-going vessels have been filled with water from the Mississippi before leaving New Orleans. Sea-captains say that this river water clears itself, and remains sweet and fresh in the tanks of vessels longer than other water.

11. The people of New Orleans use the river

water in their homes, although many people like also to drink rain-water, which is caught and preserved, in the old part of the town, in big cisterns.

12. You will enjoy a walk through the old part of the city when you come down from your post of look-out on the levee. Long ago this part of our country was owned by the French, and the French language is still spoken by many of the people. You hear a lively chatter of French when you reach the open market-place. You hear Italian, too, and Spanish, as well as our English tongue.

13. Here are men, women, and children, selling fruits and vegetables and beautiful flowers. Buy a little bunch of roses, and come for a stroll past the high garden walls which shut in many of the homes from the street.

14. Sometimes, through one of the wide, door-like gates, you catch a glimpse of flower gardens, or of children at play in a shady court, or of a lady looking from a window through a honeysuckle vine.

15. All sorts of sights may be seen in the old city, — old men selling fruit from wheelbarrows, and old women sweeping the sidewalk in front of

their little shops. Boys and girls, white, black, and brown, are everywhere, and often they are playing in the streets, in the sunshine.

16. In the business part of the city you see broader streets and finer buildings, but you will always remember the old city of New Orleans.

CHAPTER XXII.

UP THE MISSISSIPPI.

1. We have had glimpses of the Mississippi River several times in earlier journeys. Now we are going to follow the great river up to its source. We go on board a steamer at New Orleans on a pleasant morning, and ride away to the westward, with the rich vegetation of Louisiana on both sides of the stream.

2. Above New Orleans is the beautiful country of which Longfellow wrote in Evangeline. Going up the stream, you come to the place where " sweeps with majestic course the river away to the eastward."

3. On both sides of the river, all the way up

through Louisiana, are lakes and bayous, opening
from the main stream. When Evangeline and the
people with her rowed out upon one of these
bayous, —

"Over their heads the towering and tenebrous boughs of
    the cypress
  Met in a dusky arch, and trailing mosses in mid-air
  Waved like banners that hang on the walls of ancient
    cathedrals.
  Lovely the moonlight was, as it glanced and gleamed on
    the water,
  Gleamed on the columns of cypress and cedar sustaining
    the arches."

4. As the oarsmen of Evangeline's boat rowed
along in the night, one of them blew a blast on
his bugle, so that if there were other people out
upon the bayou, they would hear and guide their
boat so that neither would run upon the other in
the darkness.

5. The blast of the bugle only awoke the
echoes, and then the boatmen began to sing; and
nothing was heard on the silent water under the
overhanging trees but "the whoop of the crane
and the roar of the grim alligator."

6. At noon next day, Evangeline's boat was in a place, where, in the broad daylight, many lovely things could be seen,—

"Water-lilies in myriads rocked on the slight undulations,
　Made by the passing oars, and resplendent in beauty, the
　　lotus
　Lifted her golden crown above the heads of the boatmen.
　Faint was the air with the odorous breath of magnolia
　　blossoms,
　And with the heat of noon; and numberless sylvan islands,
　Fragrant and thickly embroidered with blossoming hedges
　　of roses,
　Near to whose shores they glided along, invited to slum-
　　ber."

7. You may wish to sleep, too, for a little time after luncheon, but your nap will be a short one. Your eyes are wide open to see all that you are passing. You see fields of sugar-cane on both sides of the river stretching away as far as your eye can reach.

8. Near the river are trees and vines, but not a rock nor a large stone is anywhere to be seen. You pass an island now and then, on the side where the current flows less swiftly.

9. After a time you pass by a place where a large stream, the Red River, flows into the Mississippi. You observe that its water is darker than that of the great river, and looks almost red before the waters mingle.

10. This is because at some distance back from its mouth it flows through dark red clay ground which crumbles off into the water and colors it and so gives the Red River its name.

11. The steamer stops at a wooden wharf. Numbers of people, many of them colored people, are waiting to see the steamer. There is a gentleman with a wide-brimmed soft hat, and a satchel in his hand. He is a planter from one of the river counties of Mississippi, and is going up to Memphis on business.

12. This is Natchez, and it is in the state of Mississippi. We cannot see all the town from the wharf. There is a high bluff rising up a little way back from the river. The business houses in the town under the hill we can see from the boat.

13. Going on up the river, after the steamer starts again, you may look back and see that there are houses and churches, and a fine park on the

bluff. This upper town is called Natchez-on-the-Hill.

14. Vicksburg is the next city at which we stop. It is also in the state of Mississippi, and it is not a long ride by train from Vicksburg to Jackson, the capital of the state. At Vicksburg casks and barrels are loaded upon the steamer, and we are told that it is cotton-seed oil.

15. You remember that the seed is separated from the cotton by the cotton-gins, and large quantities of oil, used for various purposes, are made from the seeds. Some people like cotton-seed oil for use in cookery.

16. We have now come four hundred miles from New Orleans. We are more than five hundred miles from the Gulf of Mexico, yet we have scarcely begun our journey. Our first boat-journey on the Potomac, long as it seemed, was not so long as this one has been already. You begin to realize that the Mississippi is a very large river, do you not? The Indians called it the Father of Waters.

17. One of the great branches of the Mississippi is the Arkansas River, which flows down

through the state of Arkansas. The capital of the state, Little Rock, is on its banks.

18. Not far from Little Rock, in the mountains, are the famous Hot Springs. There are more than fifty of these springs on the slope of a mountain; and invalids come great distances for the benefit which they obtain from these waters.

19. In the Ozark Mountains further north are the Eureka Springs. The water of these springs is cold and pure, and the town is very picturesque. Standing on the piazza of a hotel on the mountain side at Eureka, you can look over a pretty valley to the great pine forests beyond. Deer are still plentiful in the Ozark forests.

20. The next city we see, on our journey up the Mississippi above the mouth of the Arkansas, is Memphis. There is a good deal of smoke rising above Memphis, and from the steamer we can see many large chimneys; so you can easily guess that there are a good many mills and factories here.

21. This is the largest city between New Orleans and St. Louis, a distance of nearly twelve hundred miles; and there is no other city for a

thousand miles east or west of Memphis that is as large ; so you see it has a great deal of business to manage, — cotton and molasses to buy and send away, and all sorts of things to make or to import from the North. The lovely lawns around many of the homes in Memphis form one of the chief beauties of the city, especially as they are green all the year round.

22. On goes our steamboat, up the mile-wide river, on and on. We pass the shores of Kentucky, and we stop at Cairo, in Illinois, where the broad Ohio flows into the great river.

23. It was here that Evangeline's boat first began its southward journey. We can imagine it floating by us, as it comes down past the Ohio shore and out —

"Into the golden stream of the broad and swift Missis-
    sippi."

24. We can think that the people on a steamer we pass are going to see all that Evangeline saw, and all that our journey has showed us so far, of plume-like islands, silvery sand-bars, the houses of planters, negro-cabins, and dove-cots.

CHAPTER XXIII.

ST. LOUIS AND NORTHWARD.

AT ST. LOUIS.

1. Above the mouth of the Ohio River we find ourselves in the corn region again. East of us are the prairies of Illinois, and west of us are the lowlands and the hills of Missouri.

2. St. Louis, the largest city in Missouri, and one of the largest cities of our country, is on the west bank of the Mississippi. Our steamboat goes under a long bridge, one of the finest bridges in the world, which is built across the Mississippi at St. Louis. There are both a railroad bridge and a carriage bridge. We can stop over in St. Louis until the next steamer for the North comes, and walk over this great bridge, and see many pleasant sights in the city.

3. The public buildings in St. Louis are large and handsome, and you will enjoy a ride on the street-cars through the broad and pleasant streets where the homes of the people are built. You must go to visit the parks and the fine botanical gardens.

4. You must see the statues, the fountains, and the grain warehouses of St. Louis; and whether you wish it or not, you will see clouds of black smoke from the chimneys of the factories, where soft coal, a fuel that makes a great deal of smoke, is burned.

5. There is one great station where trains from East and West, North and South, enter. You may see cars in the Union Depot, marked for New York or San Francisco, Boston or New Orleans. St. Louis is about as far south as Washington, although it is, of course, many hundred miles west of the capital of our country.

6. It is far enough south, you see, for the fruit trees to blossom, and the grass to be green early in the spring; and the country is like a garden much earlier than in the North. Corn and sugar-cane from the farms of Missouri, lead and

iron from the mines in the Missouri hills, and fruit and vegetables from the market gardens outside the city, — all find a market here.

7. Jefferson is the capital of Missouri. It is on the Missouri River, west of St. Louis.

8. Twenty miles up the Mississippi, above St. Louis, a broad yellow river flows into the Mississippi. As we go up the stream from St. Louis on our steamboat, we see that the water of the river, which has been far from clear all the way up from New Orleans, grows more and more yellow. We know the cause of this when we see the broad flood of the Missouri, pouring its yellow waters down into the stream.

9. The Missouri is a very wide and long river, wider and longer than any other river in the country, except the river into which it flows. The reason that the water of the Missouri is so yellow may be found in the color of the clay banks through which the river runs for many hundred miles.

10. It is a very soft sort of earth, and crumbles readily into the water. The banks of the Missouri change their shape very often because they are

so soft. This is quite different from the course of rivers that force their way through a rocky country.

11. A corn farm bordering on the Missouri may gain or lose an acre of ground by the river in the course of a year or two. For sometimes the river piles up clay sediment on one side, when it crumbles and washes it away on the other side of the current further up the stream.

12. There is a large and growing city called Kansas City on the Missouri River in the western part of the state. There are many handsome public buildings and beautiful homes in Kansas City. It is a city built on bluffs of the river, and the cable-cars go up and down very steep hills.

13. As we go on up the Mississippi, above the mouth of the Missouri, we see that the water is pure and clear. We are above the clayey region. The Illinois River, the Des Moines River, and other streams bring clear water down to the broad stream upon which we are sailing. Near the mouth of the Des Moines there are rapids in the Mississippi.

14. We may go ashore at Keokuk, a town in

Iowa, and take another steamer above the rapids for St. Paul. The trees on the banks and on islands in the river are poplars and hickories instead of cypress and live oak.

15. We no longer see the long gray moss that hung on the Southern trees, but rich green moss on the ground about the trunks of the trees. High bluffs, wooded prairies, and rolling fields of oats, wheat, and barley are to be seen on the shores.

16. We see several railroad bridges over the river, as we steam on day after day. One of these great bridges crosses the Mississippi at Rock Island. This bridge is in two divisions, connected by the track, laid across the island in the middle of the river.

17. There is an arsenal on the island, and you can see the soldiers and the cannon as you pass by. It is often cold enough in winter to freeze the stream here, and people go skating and sleighing upon the ice. Davenport in Iowa and Rock Island in Illinois are the towns connected by this great railroad bridge.

18. Dubuque in Iowa, on the west bank of the river, is the next city in importance that we visit.

All around us, for a long way, in the States of
Iowa, Wisconsin, and Illinois, across the river,
there are great lead mines. The lead is brought
into Dubuque for sale and shipment.

19. Lead mining is much easier work than iron
or coal mining, as lead is often found in small
masses on or near the surface of the ground.
Boys often find the lead, and there is a good deal
of rivalry among the boys of this part of the
country in this way of earning money for Christmas or the Fourth of July.

20. At the wharf we see people busy at work in
and about the warehouses and the grain elevators.
The streets of Dubuque are terraced off, one above
another, on the high bluffs above the river. If it
is at night that we see this pretty city, we shall
not soon forget the shining of the rows of lights
on the river and their reflection in the water, like
bright stars.

21. Several hours' ride above Dubuque is the
mouth of the Wisconsin River. La Crosse, in
the State of Wisconsin, is another pretty city on
the river. Do you remember that our steamer
stopped at Milwaukee on the coast of Lake Michi-

gan, on our journey from Buffalo to Chicago, around the lakes? Milwaukee is in the eastern part of Wisconsin. Madison, the capital of the state, is in a beautiful country, west of Milwaukee.

22. We enter the wheat country. There have been wheat fields near the river, now and then, for a long distance; but not nearly so much wheat grows in any other state on the river as in Minnesota. At every town where we stop, as at Winona and at Red Wing, we see wheat and flour in barrels and bags.

23. Just before coming to Red Wing, the river broadens out into a beautiful lake. This is Lake Pepin. As our steamer goes over the smooth water just at sunset, we can scarcely realize that the current of the river is swift above and below these quiet waters. Our boat makes ripples of white as it goes onward; but at a very little distance the water is perfectly motionless.

24. You hear the loud whistle of an engine; and looking across the lake, you see a train rushing along a railroad track, close to the water's edge. It is in sight for a few moments, then turns round a wooded curve, and is gone.

CHAPTER XXIV.

MINNESOTA AND THE DAKOTAS.

1. After our next week of travel up the river from New Orleans, we are glad to reach St. Paul. This pleasant city is the capital of Minnesota, and the large steamboats can go no further up the river. The falls of St. Anthony are a few miles above St. Paul, and the city of Minneapolis is built beside the falls on both banks of the river.

2. The Mississippi is much narrower here, as you may well imagine, than it is away down stream below where it has been fed by other large rivers. But it is even here a most useful river. The waters of the falls of St. Anthony have made flour from wheat in the flouring mills of Minneapolis for many years.

3. Both St. Paul and Minneapolis have grown so fast since 1880 that they are now almost like one large city. Between them is a fine park, with beautiful drives and promenades, and at the famous falls of Minnehaha, about midway, there is a charming rocky glen.

4. Both cities are picturesque; for both are built on the bluffs above the river. The country round about has many lovely lakes and wooded drives. From a distance you can see the spires of churches, the college buildings, and the tall grain elevators where millions of bushels of wheat are stored.

5. Minnesota, like the states west of it, North Dakota and South Dakota, is celebrated for its great wheat fields. Some of these fields are larger than the big pasture on the Texas ranch, of which we have already spoken.

6. In Dakota, there are fields of wheat so large that you could follow the reaper in one direction a full half day before it would turn to cut the next swath of grain. Wheat grows on almost all of the smaller farms, too; so you see where a good deal of the flour for bread comes from.

7. The Missouri River flows down through the central part of both Dakotas, and along its upper waters are many vast cattle ranges. But it is cold for the cattle that run out of doors all winter.

8. The winter weather in these new Northern states is very severe; cold, blinding storms of snow,

A DAKOTA WHEAT FIELD.

called blizzards, come down upon the great plains,
and in them people and animals often lose their
lives when away from shelter.

9. In St. Paul the biting cold is made a source of pleasure. A great "ice palace" is built every winter, and it is a fine sight whether glittering in the sunshine by day, or in the electric light by night.

10. Sleigh-bells make the winter merry; and as the air is very dry and light, people do not mind the cold so much as in places where there is more dampness in the cold air, as is the case on the sea-shore, or the shores of the great lakes.

11. Lake Superior is northeast of Minnesota. It is one of the great lakes which we did not see on our journey from Buffalo to Chicago. It is the largest of all the great lakes,—much larger than either Lake Michigan or Lake Huron, and twice as large as Lake Erie and Lake Ontario together.

12. If the States of Massachusetts and Connecticut were islands in this great inland sea, nearly two-thirds of its blue waters would still be left about the islands to reflect the sky.

13. Its shores are broken by many grand cliffs, and people travel long distances to see the high walls of red sandstone, called the Pictured Rocks, on the southern shore of Lake Superior.

14. In Longfellow's Hiawatha you may read
many wonderful stories of the land near Gitchee
Gumee, the shining "big sea-water," as the
Indians called Lake Superior. You can read how
Hiawatha went fishing on the lake all alone in his
birch canoe.

15.   "Through the clear transparent water
        He could see the fishes swimming
        Far down in the depths below him ;
        Saw the yellow perch, the Sahwa,
        Like a sunbeam in the water,
        Saw the Shawgashee, the craw-fish,
        Like a spider on the bottom,
        On the white and sandy bottom."

16. Hiawatha wished to catch a 'sturgeon, so
when the pike and the sun-fish came to his bait,
he shouted to them to go away, for he could see
the sturgeon "fanning slowly in the water." When
you read the story you will learn what happened
when at last the big fish came up to the surface.

17. Enormous sturgeon are found in Lake Superior. .You can see them in the markets of
Duluth, a city at the head of the lake. Duluth
is not far from rich copper mines near the shores

of the lake. The eastern end of the Northern Pacific Railroad, which extends across Dakota and still westward across the Northern states of our country to the Pacific Ocean, is at Duluth.

18. Let us enter a train on this railroad at Duluth, for a short ride through fine forests, past tamarack swamps and fields of wheat, to the town of Brainerd. Here we are once more at the Mississippi River, now a clear stream much narrower than when we saw it at Minneapolis, a hundred miles south.

19. At Brainerd we will get into a good row-boat, and row away to the north to find the source of the Mississippi. The river grows narrower and narrower as we go on.

20. By and by we enter a beautiful, clear, little lake, then another, and still another, as our boat goes on through the narrow streams.

21. Wild ducks in great numbers fly over our heads. On the shores of one of the lakes we see several deer, which look at us shyly before they bound away into the forest.

22. It takes us several days to go through the chain of lakes which lead to the one we have

come so far to see. On the shores of Lake Itasca we at last eat our dinner of broiled fish, thinking that this very fish lived but yesterday in the water before us, some of whose drops will find their way to the salt water of the Gulf of Mexico, nearly three thousand miles away.

CHAPTER XXV.

FROM DAVENPORT TO DENVER.

1. You remember passing the city of Davenport on the Mississippi River at Rock Island. We will bid good by to the Father of Waters there, and take a train for places still farther west. All day long we shall be riding over the rolling prairies of Iowa. You cannot see as far on these rolling prairies as you can on those where no swell of ground breaks the landscape.

2. You would not find much difference between Iowa and Illinois, were it not that the prairie-lands here are not usually so flat as those in Illinois. But you see fields of corn and of oats, as in Illinois. Cattle roam over the great pastures, and

there are beautiful orchards of apples and fine gardens in and about the towns that you pass.

3. Des Moines, the capital of Iowa, is one of the cities we see on this journey. It is a bright, busy city, situated on the largest river in Iowa, the Des Moines River. Council Bluffs is on the bluffs above the Missouri River, in the western part of the state. Here is a great railroad bridge, and the trains of many railroads from every direction cross the river between Council Bluffs and Omaha.

4. After crossing the Missouri, we are in the State of Nebraska. Omaha is the largest city, and from the bluffs on which it is built, we can see a long distance over the prairies which stretch away to the westward.

5. The Platte River flowing from the west, comes all the way across the state. When men first began to cross the plains to California in wagons, they always drove along the banks of the Platte River; for here they were sure of finding food for their horses and oxen.

6. There were no railroads in this part of the country then, and no towns. All of these

pretty towns have grown up since the railroads were built west of the Missouri River.

7. The railroads have made the plains of Nebraska neighbors to the hills of Maine. Whenever railroads have been built through the great fertile plains of the West, towns have soon appeared. Lincoln, the capital of Nebraska, is one of the pleasant cities on our way. We see a fine Capitol building of white stone, which reminds us of the one at Washington, although, of course, it is not so large.

8. A party of people, going on a pleasure journey to Colorado Springs, come into our car at Lincoln. A boy in the party can tell you a good many interesting things about this country. He has never seen a mountain, he says, but he is going to see one now. He has never seen any trees that were not planted, except cotton-wood trees. There are many "tree farms" on these plains.

9. The government has given lands to people who would plant a certain number of trees and take care of them. You see from the car window groups of maples and poplars, which were planted by people whom he knows.

10. The towns are fewer and smaller, and it is further and further between them, as we go on west of Lincoln. But by and by we leave the wide plains of Nebraska. We are approaching the mountain country of Colorado, and our engines pull our train up the long grades toward the beautiful city of Denver.

11. We are nearly a mile higher up in the air here than in any city we have yet visited. But we should not think of this unless some one told us; so we walk about the broad, handsome streets, and look at the public buildings and fine homes.

12. This city has grown very rapidly, like many of the large Western cities; and none of the old people who live there now were born in Denver, because there was no town there at all when they were boys and girls.

13. Wherever you go in this city you have beautiful views of mountain peaks around you. We are now at the Rocky Mountains. Between us and the Appalachian Mountains lies the great valley of the Mississippi, with many beautiful rivers flowing towards it from the mountains on the east, and from those on the west.

THE DENVER HIGH SCHOOL.

14. Away to the south we can see a high mountain, with snow upon its summit. It is Pike's Peak. People who visit Denver sometimes speak of driving over to the mountain in the morning, and are surprised when they are told that it is seventy-five miles away.

15. The air is very clear and light, and the mountain seems very much nearer. Boys sometimes feel sure that they could walk over to it, if they were allowed to do so.

CHAPTER XXVI.

KANSAS AND THE INDIAN TERRITORY.

1. South of Nebraska is the great prairie State of Kansas. If you were to go from Topeka, the capital, westward to Colorado, you would go over wide, treeless prairies, as in Nebraska. In the western part of the state there are plains unfenced for a hundred miles.

2. You may ride for hours, and not see a fence nor a house. But in the eastern part of the state, you might travel about in a country which looks

much like Illinois, or Indiana, or any of the northern states of the Mississippi Valley.

3. Once a little girl whose home was in Maine was taken by her aunt on a journey to California. She had promised her mother to send a postal card home every day. But she thought all of the country looked the same, and there was nothing to write. "It looks just like Maine," she wrote on her postal card every day for the first four days.

4. When she was near Lawrence in Kansas, some one in the car asked her if she did not think the prairies looked different from Maine. She said, "I have not seen any prairies; nothing but fields."

5. But when she saw the great plains in Western Kansas, she wrote on her postal card, "It isn't a bit like Maine. I can look away forever and ever, and see no fences." Even then she was disappointed, because she saw no buffaloes on the plains. They have all been killed since the railroads were built in every direction over the country where they used to roam.

6. Leavenworth and Atchison are two other cities of Kansas, both in the northeastern part of

the state, not far from Kansas City, which is just over the boundary in Missouri.

7. The Kansas Emigrants is the name of one of Whittier's poems, which boys and girls in the Kansas schools know by heart. Here are three of the stanzas : —

8. "We cross the prairie as of old
    The pilgrims crossed the sea,
    To make the West, as they the East,
    The homestead of the free!

9. "We go to plant her common schools
    On distant prairie swells,
    And give the Sabbaths of her wild
    The music of her bells.

10. "We'll tread the prairie as of old
    Our fathers sailed the sea,
    And make the West, as they the East,
    The homestead of the free!"

11. In the southern part of the state, coal is found, and Indian corn, tall and abundant, grows on the rich lands along the rivers. Fort Scott is one of the oldest and most pleasant towns in the state. Not far from Fort Scott you enter the Indian Territory.

12. This is not one of the states, nor is it like some other territories of which we shall read. It is a country owned by the Indians. Our government at Washington set apart this beautiful country, larger than all New England, for the Indians. Part of it has been bought of the Indians by the government; and white people may now own lands in Oklahoma, which not long ago belonged to the Indians exclusively.

13. It is a very rich and pretty country where the Indians live. Many sorts of delicious fruits grow wild here. The raspberries, blackberries, strawberries, and plums, that are found in the woods, are not so large as the cultivated ones you have seen, but they are very good indeed, and have a fine flavor.

14. You may be sure a Cherokee boy would think you very foolish if you preferred the big strawberries of the gardens to the sweet little wild ones that grow on the sunny sides of the knolls.

15. There are no large cities in the Indian country; but in the parts which have been opened to white people, there are a number of new and growing towns along the Santa Fé Railroad.

CHAPTER XXVII.

IN THE ROCKY MOUNTAINS.

1. We have had a glimpse of one mountain city, beautiful Denver, with its fine new buildings and handsome streets. Denver is in Colorado, the state which came into the Union in 1876, and so is called the Centennial State. New Mexico, south of Colorado, has not yet been admitted as a state; it is called a territory.

2. Santa Fé, the capital of New Mexico, is not one of the fine new cities of the West. It is interesting because it is old. Long before there were any railroads west of the Mississippi River, there was a town here, built by people who came from Mexico, and who spoke the Spanish language. Most of the people speak Spanish still; although since the railroad was built up to the old town, people from Missouri and other states have gone there to live.

3. We will take a short drive on the hill overlooking the town. On our way, we meet two or three boys driving a pair of small mules, loaded

with great panniers of wood. This is the way most of the wood used in the town is brought in from the forests on the mountains.

4. From our outlook on the hill, we can see the new State House and the fine new Ramona School for Indian boys and girls. There are a few fine homes, but most of the town is of one-story adobe houses. We drive back to the plaza, or public square, in the centre of the town.

5. Let us go down that narrow street, and look at the queer, picturesque houses. The adobe is a sort of brick dried in the sun, and has the color of dry clay. Many of the houses have blue doors, or vines growing over them, so that they do not seem to be all of the same color.

6. There is a group of Mexican children at play in the garden beside the house. You see the little brown things swinging under the cedar-trees. You go into a shop where all sorts of odd and interesting trinkets, made by Indians, are for sale, and an Indian, in the gayest costume possible, dances and sings to amuse you. You go up to the old Spanish Church, and see a bell which was made in Spain hundreds of years ago.

7. The people in New Mexico do not work so hard as the people in most parts of our country.

IN THE ROCKY MOUNTAINS.

There are great sheep ranches throughout the territory; and although there are a few good farms, so much of the state is covered by mountains, hills, and dry plains, that but little grain and fruit are grown.

8. One of the most pleasant places in all the mountains is Las Vegas, where there are hot springs. You will not find the water hot enough to burn your mouth when you taste it; but it is hot enough to cause vapor to rise from the different springs.

9. In Colorado, north of New Mexico, are many beautiful mountain towns. Manitou and Colorado Springs are much visited by travellers. The mountains are very high in Colorado. There are about two hundred very high peaks in the state; Pike's Peak, which we saw from Denver, is the most famous. The mountain ranges in Colorado enclose three great plateaus called parks.

10. Of course they are larger than any parks made near cities, and the mountains that surround them make very high fences. These parks have fertile soil, and here are some of the best farms in Colorado. The fruit that grows on these highland farms is firm and fine, and the cattle and sheep find tender wild grasses almost all the year round.

11. You might spend the entire summer travelling in the Rocky Mountains in Colorado, and you would not see all the beauties of the scenery. On the narrow gauge railroad, west of Denver, there are rocks and gorges, mountain heights and lonely valleys to be seen, more wonderful than it is possible to imagine. The Royal Gorge is famous for its noble scenery.

12. There are many great mines of gold and silver in Colorado, which yield millions of dollars every year.

CHAPTER XXVIII.

OUR NATIONAL PARKS.

1. The new state of Wyoming is north of Colorado. In the northwest corner of Wyoming is a park more interesting and far more wonderful than the parks of Colorado. This is the Yellowstone National Park, set apart by the government at Washington for our pleasure, and owned by all the country. As this park belongs to the nation, it is, of course, an immense one. It is larger than some of the Eastern states.

2. If we were going to visit the wonderful Yellowstone region, we should go on a railroad which approaches the park from Montana, another great northern state. Our train takes us along the banks of the Yellowstone River.

3. We see wild ducks on the shores of the clear water, and some one tells us that the river is full of trout and grayling. We can see the snow on the high mountains to the east, and on the west, low, curiously shaped volcanic domes and peaks.

4. At the village of Cinnabar, near a high mountain with red cliffs, the railroad ends. We must go up the river-bank now to the Mammoth Hot Springs in a stage-coach. Here we begin to see the wonders of the Yellowstone wonder-land. On four terraces are the fifty-two hot springs. Over these terraces the water falls in little brooks and cascades.

5. All sorts of bright and lovely colors are to be seen around these boiling springs. The water itself is very clear and transparent, and blue as a turquoise.

6. You will wish to gather from the little streams that flow from the boiling springs some

of the silky fibres that quiver in the water, like sea-mosses in a pool of salt water.

7. From the hotel at Mammoth Hot Springs we go up to the geysers in mountain wagons. Sometimes, however, people prefer to go on horseback. Geysers are hot springs that bubble, seethe, and throw hot water in great columns into the air.

8. We see mud springs on our way, and a dozen odd, high chimneys of old geysers which are no longer active. You are sure to notice the one that looks like an old man who has lost his head.

9. As we go on, we find springs of all kinds, — hundreds of them. You are soon tired of trying to count them. But the wonder of wonders appears when you first see a geyser throwing a column of boiling water into the air higher than any church steeple that you ever saw. All around the Excelsior Geyser is a wide basin of boiling water, and the streams which come from it are colored like rainbows.

10. You walk to the Grand Prismatic Spring, not far from the Excelsior Geyser, and in the ground you see a big basin of blue, boiling water,

fading into green around the sides. There is a
shallower basin around this one, in which you can
count all the colors of the rainbow.

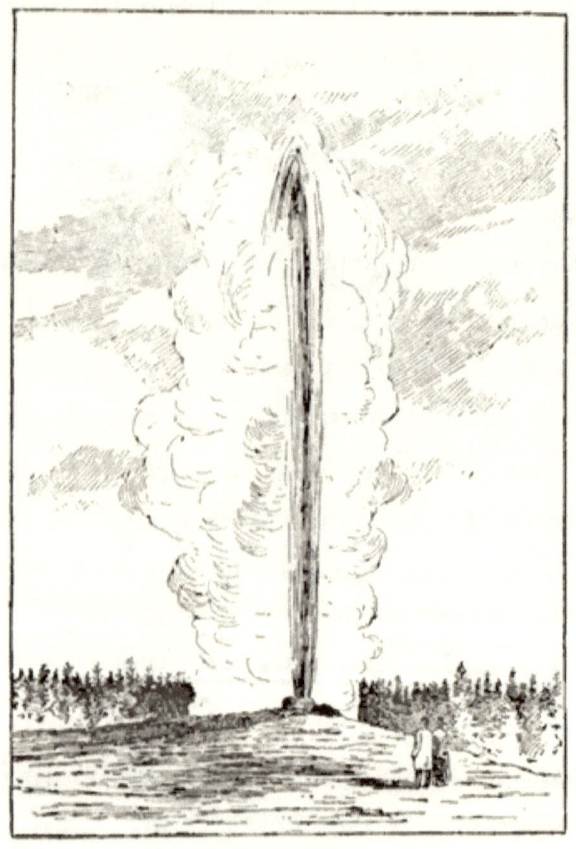

OLD FAITHFUL.

11. We have now only begun to see the geysers.
There are dozens more in the upper Geyser Basin.
One is called Old Faithful, because it sends up its

column of boiling water regularly once an hour. The eruption lasts about five minutes.

12. It begins with a few bubbles, but soon boils violently. This lasts for a little while; then comes a puff, and up goes jet after jet, with a roar like thunder; and the steam rushes up three times as high as the hot water.

13. The Giantess sends forth its eruptions about once in two weeks. People sometimes toss hand-kerchiefs into it for sport, and after a while they are tossed out again by the bubbling water; sometimes torn.

14. There are many other wonderful and beau-tiful sights to be seen in our National Park. The Yellowstone Falls are more beautiful, although not so grand, as Niagara.

15. You will understand, as you go up the Grand Cañon between high walls of rock, why this is called the Yellowstone country. For the water, dripping through the rocks, has given them in many places the color of gold; although you will see on the rocky walls and columns every other color of the rainbow, all rich and brilliant as the sunset sky.

CHAPTER XXIX.

ACROSS THE DESERT.

1. The prairies and the plains of our country have become well known to us in earlier chapters. You have seen them rich with farms of corn and wheat; you have seen numbers of cattle, horses, and sheep, roaming over their pastures. You have seen many rivers, valleys, mountains, and cities. Now we are to see the sandy deserts.

2. There is a vast amount of land, between the east and west coasts of our country, where no plants grow. But in many places where nothing grows now there will by and by be farms producing abundant fruit and grain. For in Arizona and in the desert parts of California there are already acres upon acres of dry land which has been turned into fine farms by irrigation.

3. In those states where there is plenty of rain, few boys and girls know the meaning of the word irrigation. But in places where very little rain falls all the year round, irrigation is one of the common words that children learn to speak.

4. There are irrigating ditches that bring water from some distant river or reservoir, into everybody's garden. Boys who sail their boats on the irrigating ditches, or build bridges over them, soon understand that irrigation is the method of giving water to plants, grains, and trees, so as to make them grow when there is no rain.

5. Arizona does not consist entirely of these dry lands. Along the rivers there is soil that is rich and fertile. Wherever you find a town or city here, you may be sure that it is near a river. But you may ride for miles in the territory and scarcely see a creek.

6. Out of the wide, dry plain high mountains rise here and there, which stand out singly and alone, their rugged summits almost always covered with snow. These great solitary cones seem higher than mountains of the same height that stand in groups or chains.

7. The cañons of the Colorado River are the wonder of this part of the world. The broad, deep river, coming down from distant mountains, forces its way for two hundred miles between walls of stone as high as mountains.

8. If you were brave enough to attempt the descent through one of the cañons by boat, you would find yourself at times almost shut away from daylight, so high are the walls on each side of the rushing river. Call as loudly as you could, your voice would not be heard, even if some one were walking on the stony banks, thousands of feet above you.

9. When you come out upon the Mojave desert, as you go westward on the train again, you see land upon which nothing grows. Even the sage-bush, which grew upon the Arizona plains, is gone, and there is only barren sand for a stretch of nearly two hundred miles.

10. It is intensely hot on the Mojave desert in summer. Nobody lives there except the tele-graph operators, the station agents needed by the railroad, and the men who keep the track in order. All their food and water is brought to them on the train, as it passes by. Their houses are made of plain, unplastered boards; for it is never cold in the Mojave country, not even in the dead of winter.

11. Before you come to the land of grass and

trees again, the train stops at a town larger than any which you have passed for a very long distance. This is Daggett, which is situated not far from the gold mines at Calico. You can see the barren-looking mountains in the distance, where the gold is found.

12. The huge piles of old tin-cans lying about the track show you where most of the food of the people comes from. Gardens and fruit-trees do not flourish here; and fresh vegetables and fruit are not common luxuries, for they must be brought from a long distance.

13. By and by you come to a new town, laid out with avenues of palms, and with orange-trees planted about the few houses in the place. Then you see that irrigation will do wonders even in the sand. At last you reach the town of San Bernandino, in California, and the wide desert is behind you.

14. In Nevada, the state north of the Mojave region, there are many large desert tracts of land. The Humboldt desert is crossed by the Union Pacific, the first of all the great railroads which have been built across the continent. There are

barren plains for a long way east of the Humboldt desert.

15. A little girl whose home is in California often goes across the country all the way from California to Washington with her father, who is a member of the government at the national capital.

16. She described this part of the country, by saying, " You ride for a thousand miles and never see a single tree; the desolation makes you feel almost homesick; and by the time you get to the place where the trees grow again you have almost forgotten how they look."

17. There is a low bush called the sage-bush which grows in some parts of these arid plains. There is very little water to be found here, and this tastes too strong of alkali to be very good to drink.

18. But even this dry region has some pleasant things about it; and the people who live on the plains will tell you that nowhere else in all our country will you breathe air so pure and dry, nor see such blue sky by day, nor so many stars at night.

CHAPTER XXX.

SALT LAKES AND SILVER MINES.

1. In the northern part of the territory of Utah there is a lake almost half as large as Lake Ontario, in which the water is salter than the water of the ocean. Rivers flow into it, but none flow from it, as they do from fresh-water lakes, and fishes do not live in it. It is not a deep lake, like the great lakes of the north. Indeed, you could wade about in it in many places, and you would not be at all afraid to go bathing in its shallower water.

2. But you would never forget it if you once tried to dive or swim in Salt Lake. For the water stings the face of those who dive; and it is so buoyant that it fairly tips over many good swimmers who try to swim in the lake.

3. People who visit the lake go on making experiments, although they are told that they will be unpleasant. Wild geese, ducks, and gulls come here in immense flocks. You can see them flying over the islands.

4. This lake, called Great Salt Lake, is the largest salt lake in our country; but there are many smaller ones in different parts of the country. They are to be found in Utah, in New Mexico, in Texas, and in California. But most of the salt which we use comes from the salt springs in more eastern states, — in New York, Michigan, Ohio, and West Virginia.

5. Salt Lake City, the capital of Utah, is near the lake. This is the home of the Mormons. There are pleasant valleys not far away, in the Wahsatch Mountains, where there are many farms made fertile by irrigation.

6. Very fine potatoes are grown in these valleys. These, with a great deal of butter and millions of dozens of eggs, are sent over the Humboldt desert and the Sierra Nevada Mountains, to supply the markets of the largest city west of the Rocky Mountains, — San Francisco.

7. South of the Humboldt desert, in Nevada, there are several cities which have grown up around the silver mines of this part of the world. Virginia City is one of these, and not far south of it is Carson, the capital of Nevada.

8. Great fortunes have been made from the mines near Virginia City. Some of the shafts are sunk deep down into the ground. The silver is found in lodes, or veins, in the mountain mines. The miners work at one of these as long as there is any silver to be found; then the mine is sunk deeper, and still the work goes on.

9. More than twenty-three million dollars' worth of gold and silver was taken from one lode in one year when these mines were first discovered.

CHAPTER XXXI.

ALASKA.

1. Away to the north is Alaska, a great territory, which is not shown on all of the maps because it is separated from the rest of the country by a part of British America. Alaska is a very large territory, but not many white people live in it yet. There are still many Indians in the territory, for a great deal of it is cold and not suited for pleasant homes.

2. But there are opportunities for making

money, which cause people to go to Alaska. Probably after the territories of New Mexico and Arizona have people enough living in them to entitle them to be admitted into the Union as states, instead of remaining territories, Alaska will ask to come into the Union as a state too. But this territory will not become a state for many years yet.

3. Alaska is a very large territory. If you could put Texas, California, and all the New England States into it, you would still have room for Illinois and Ohio. If you could sail around the coast of Alaska you would find it a very long journey indeed; for this territory has a longer coast-line than all of the states on the Atlantic coast, the Gulf of Mexico, and the Pacific Ocean.

4. But few people travel or live in Alaska except along the southern coast; for it is very cold in the north of the territory, which is open to the cold winds from the Arctic Ocean with its great icebergs.

5. Cape Barrow, extending into the Arctic Ocean, is the most northern point of land belonging to the United States. It is always winter

there, and nothing will grow. But in the southern part of the territory, it is warm and pleasant in the summer, and the winters are no colder than in Illinois or in Maine.

6. Sitka is the capital, and Juneau is one of the other towns. Gold, coal, and great quantities of sulphur come from Alaska. Ice and lumber are shipped to California; but the chief business of the people is catching animals for their furs, and fishing and whaling.

7. Otters and beavers are numerous, and seals, from whose fur sealskin cloaks, muffs, and caps are made, are caught along the coast. Whaling-vessels go from the New England shores to Alaska, and bring home oil and bones of the whales. There are millions and millions of cod in these waters and all the way down the west coast.

8. There are forty or fifty large fish-canning establishments on the mainland and on the islands. Salmon are packed in tin cans for shipment to distant markets. Some Indians find occupation in these places, and many Chinese. At Kesa-an Bay large quantities of salmon are caught.

9. Says Mr. Ballou, in his book, The New El
Dorado, " No spot on the coast is more famous for
the abundance and excellency of its salmon; at
certain seasons the waters of the bay swarm with
them.   Here is a large cannery, where native
women do most of the indoor work.   Two thousand barrels of salted salmon, independent of canning, were shipped from there in one year.

10. "The salmon are so plenty in the regular
season, that an Indian will sometimes deliver at
the cannery three or four canoe loads in a single
day. They are mostly caught by net or seine,
but often during the height of the season the
natives absolutely shovel the salmon out of the
water to the shore with their paddle blades.

11. " The bears ·know very well when the run
of salmon commences, and that there are certain
quiet inlets where the fish are sure to get crowded
and jammed, so that Bruin has only to reach out
his paws and draw one after another to the shore
and eat his fill."   There are thousands and thousands of bears, grizzly, cinnamon, and black, in
Alaska.

12. There are two large glaciers or ice-rivers in

Takou Inlet. One comes down to the sea, and icebergs often slide from it into the deep water. A thousand streams fed by ice and snow pour into the bay from the surrounding mountains. The music of falling water is the only sound.

13. Millions of white, wild water-fowl rise up from these bays, when the steamer comes whistling in. The scenery is wonderfully impressive. The colors of sky and sea are reflected on the glittering glaciers. Sometimes people travelling up the coast in pleasant, sunny weather see a terrible snow-storm raging on the high mountains of the mainland.

CHAPTER XXXII.

NEW STATES AND DOWN THE COAST.

1. Washington is the most northerly state on the west coast of our country. It is a new state, like North Dakota, South Dakota, and Montana, and came into the Union with them in 1889.

2. The President chose Washington's birthday, February 22, as the day for signing the bill for

the admission of these four new states. Wyoming and Idaho were not admitted till 1890.

3. In the Dakotas, as we have already seen, there are great wheat farms. There are also immense cattle ranges extending into Montana. The name Montana shows that it is a mountain state. Several chains of mountains cross the state, and the western part of it is covered with a network of low mountains. Between these ranges there are many fertile and pleasant valleys.

4. East of the great divide, these valleys broaden out like great trumpets. They become plateaus and rolling prairies, and at last towards the northeast is an immense plain where herds of cattle roam over the wide ranges.

5. Gold and silver in great quantities are found in Montana. More gold has been found in its hills and valleys than in any other state except California. There is also a great deal of copper in Montana. .

6. People travelling to the Pacific coast, by the northern route, cross Montana and the northern part of Idaho on their way to the State of Washington. A great inlet of the Pacific Ocean, called

Puget Sound, forms a large part of the coast of Washington. This sound extends eighty miles southward into the land.

7. On the shores of Puget Sound are several flourishing, new cities; among which are Tacoma, Seattle, and Port Townsend. Hundreds of people are going to the Puget Sound country every month. Spokane Falls is in the eastern part of the state. Olympia is the capital.

8. Walla Walla is one of the oldest towns in all the far west. It is situated inland, near the Oregon boundary, and in the centre of a good wheat-growing country. The houses and public buildings have been built for years, and so give the place an air of settled life.

9. If you should travel in Washington, you would find people busy in farming, mining, and fishing, and in making lumber. You would see fields of wheat, barley, and potatoes, and fine apple orchards. You would travel through vast forests of fir, and you would see, even on a hot summer's day, the snow on the high mountains of the Cascade Range.

10. The Columbia River, one of the largest

rivers in the United States, separates the state
of Oregon from the state of Washington. It flows
down through the Cascade Mountains, then through
the Coast Mountains to the Pacific Ocean. Pacific
means peaceful. There are seldom such terrible storms off our West coast as there are off
the Atlantic shores.

11. If you look at the map, you will see that
there are very few islands all the way from Cape
Flattery off Puget Sound, to San Diego,—not near
so many as there are between Maine and Florida.
There are no islands of any considerable size off
the coast of Oregon.

12. Ocean steamers go up the Columbia River
and the Willamette to Portland, the largest city
in Oregon. Here is the great shipping point for
the salmon caught in the Columbia River. Flour
and wheat, wool and lumber are also shipped from
Portland.

13. It is never very cold in Eastern Oregon, so
that the sheep on the great sheep ranches can feed
out of doors all the year around, as in Texas. In
this part of the state there are immense forests of
redwood. The trees grow to a great size; but

beyond the mountains, are vast dry plains, like those in Nevada, where nothing but stunted bushes will grow.

14. All the way down the coast, from Portland to San Francisco, you can see the low peaks of the Coast Mountains. Your steamer stops at one or two ports in the redwood country, and you see the great piles of lumber in the lumber-yards.

15. Before sailing through the Golden Gate, as the entrance to

NEAR SAN DIEGO.

San Francisco Bay is called, you pass the Farallon Islands. The steamer goes on between the high points that guard the narrow entrance, and into the broad and beautiful bay to the city's wharf.

16. On the California coast, south of San Francisco, there are many interesting towns. It would be pleasant to visit them all. Monterey, on the Bay of Monterey, is a seashore town, where many Californians spend the summers, in order to be away from the heat of the valleys, or from the cold winds that blow every afternoon in San Francisco.

17. On the Atlantic coast the cool breezes in the summer come from the east, but on the Pacific coast the cool summer breezes come from the west. In both cases the cool winds come from the ocean; for, you know, the ocean is colder than the land in summer, and this makes the sea breezes colder than the land breezes.

18. Across the bay from Monterey, is Santa Cruz, a pleasant little city on a circle of wooded hills. Los Angeles, in Southern California, is a little way inland, but has a good port. As you sail into San Diego Bay, you will be delighted with the beauty of Coronado Beach, and not far to the south you will see the Mexican Hills.

CHAPTER XXXIII.

CALIFORNIAN VALLEYS.

1. As we have seen, the Coast Range of mountains extends along the entire western coast of California. These are low mountains, not nearly so high as the Sierra Nevada Mountains, which extend from the Mojave Desert to the Cascade Mountains of Oregon. Between the Sierras and the Coast Range, lie the great California valleys famous for fruit and for wheat. The San Bernandino and San Gabriel Valleys in the south are distinct from these, and here is the great orange country.

2. As you ride up the San Gabriel Valley, you see thousands of new orange-groves. You come to Riverside and find nearly everybody busy with the growing or the sending away of oranges and raisins. You see vineyards where the grape-vines are trimmed away every year, until nothing is left but the trunk.

3. Everything grows so fast here that it would not be possible to walk about in the vineyards,

if the vines were trimmed as little as in colder
states. It is never cold in the California valleys.
There are no winters of ice and snow. During
the winter there are rains which make the fields
and gardens green and beautiful, and roses bloom
out of doors all the year round.

4. In the summer no rain falls, and it is very
hot and dusty. But there is always a cool

ON THE SOUTHERN PACIFIC RAILROAD.

wind at night, so that the people do not mind
the heat of the days so much.

5. The San Joaquin Valley is a vast ranch
country on both sides of the San Joaquin River.
Into this broad river, a smaller river, called the

Merced, flows down from the Sierras. Up in the mountains the Merced has a picturesque journey through the famous Yosemite Valley.

6. Three high and lovely waterfalls are formed by the little river in its plunges down the mountain sides. The valley is not long and not wide. The high rocks and mountains of Yosemite are in strange and wonderful forms. The Sentinel, and Cathedral Rock, are names which show what their forms suggest; but no one can have much idea of the noble beauty of the scenery without seeing Yosemite.

7. People who have travelled around the world, and have seen and praised many beautiful sights, say, when they come to Yosemite, that they can think of no words to express their feelings of admiration and awe, as they first turn the mountain corner from which they look upon the valley.

8. The people whose home is in Yosemite, are snowed in for months at a time during the winter, for there are snow-storms in the high Sierra valleys when the lowland valleys of California are full of flowers and growing grain. But during

the spring and summer there are always parties
of people coming up to stay in the hotel or to
camp in the mountain pleasure-ground; for the

IN THE YOSEMITE.

valley belongs to the state of California. It is
a state park, just as the National Park in Wyoming belongs to all of the United States.

9. In the late summer, when the snows are melted off the mountains higher still in the range, there is little water for the waterfalls. They grow much smaller than they are in the spring, when the famous valley is in all its beauty, as if ready to be seen by the visitors who come from all parts of the world.

10. There is a little valley, also in the Sierras, more than a hundred miles north of Yosemite, in which all the world was once interested. This is Coloma, in El Dorado County, where the first gold in California was discovered many years ago. Most of the gold has long ago been taken from the Coloma placers, and there are fruit ranches now in the little valley, where fine mountain peaches, plums, and apricots grow.

11. These fruits are sent east to Chicago, New York, and Boston, from stations on the Union Pacific Railroad, the first railroad built across our continent. On every fruit ranch in this little valley, there are also a great many rose-bushes, and all the spring and summer the air is sweet with their fragrance.

12. Higher up in the Sierras, there are many

gold mines, where fortunes are still taken from
the quartz. Thousands of dollars worth of gold
are sent from each of them down to the government mint at San Francisco, to be made into

MOUNT SHASTA.

money. Silver and copper are also mined in the
California Sierras. And it is near these mountains, you remember, on the Nevada side, that
the great silver mines are found.

13. Sacramento, the capital of California, is
on the Sacramento River. Steamers come up

this broad river past the grain fields and the fruit ranches of the Sacramento Valley from San Francisco. From one of these river steamers, you can see, away to the west, the low purple peaks of the Coast Range, and away to the east, the snowy summits of the Sierras, looking like clouds against the sky. On either side of the river are the plains, broad and level as an Illinois prairie. North of the city, half way to Oregon, is the Shasta region and beautiful Mount Shasta.

14. If you were in Santa Cruz, the pretty little city we had a glimpse of from the ocean as we passed Monterey Bay, and wished to go to San Francisco, you would have your choice of two delightful journeys. If you went up to San Francisco Bay over the narrow gauge road, you would go through the picturesque Santa Cruz Mountains, and see a group of big redwood trees. You would pass the apricot orchards of Los Gatos, and see in the distance the heights of New Almaden, where there is one of the largest mines of quicksilver in the world.

15. If it happened to be a hot summer day, you might think that a great deal of the quicksilver

must be used in making thermometers for use in this lovely Santa Clara Valley. You would have glimpses of San José, its normal school, and the

IN A VINEYARD.

beautiful drive to Santa Clara, two miles away.

16. In the distance you would see Mount Hamilton where there is an immense telescope. It does not rain here during the entire summer, and nowhere is there so fine an opportunity to study the stars as on Mount Hamilton.

17. On goes the train, and you see from the windows broad fields of grain, vineyards, and orchards of peaches as well as of almonds and apricots. You pass Palo Alto and the line of oak groves below the bay. Your train reaches Oakland. You go on board a ferry-boat and ride over the blue waters of the bay to San Francisco.

CHAPTER XXXIV.

IN SAN FRANCISCO.

1. When you come out of the ferry station in San Francisco, you see a number of cable-cars waiting on the turn-table at the end of the street. Cable-cars were used in San Francisco before they were used anywhere else. The man who invented them thought that there ought to be some way of going up and down the steep hills on which much of the city is built, and these fast-going cars are the result of his thought.

2. We will take a ride on one; but first let us walk a short distance up the broad business street which ends at the ferry station. This is Market

Street. You see high business blocks that look very much like the tall stone buildings of New York or Chicago. But they are not of stone. Nearly all of them are built of wood and are painted to look like stone.

3. We see the largest hotel in the world, and can scarcely believe that it is all made of wood. We walk over to California Street, get upon a cable-car, and ride up a high hill which is terraced off by the cross streets, and all of the costly homes that we see are built of wood.

4. There are sometimes earthquakes in California, and if a house is to be shaken down, there is less danger for its occupants if it is built of some light material. There has not been a very severe earthquake in San Francisco for many years, and some of the newer buildings are of stone or brick.

5. You notice that all of the houses have bay windows, which, on some of them, extend all the way to the roof. The San Franciscans keep warm by the sun. It is not necessary to warm the buildings with furnaces, and if there are plenty of sunny windows in homes, business buildings,

and in schoolhouses, there are not many weeks in the year when people need fires in the stoves or grates. Sunny rooms are almost as necessary in the summer months as during the cold, rainy season, for every afternoon a chilly wind blows across the city from the mountains.

6. It is not at all uncommon to see a lady wearing a sealskin cloak, and carrying a parasol on a July afternoon; and men often wear thick overcoats and straw hats in the summer. Then, too, you may see ladies wearing lace shawls and men working with their coats off on a sunny day in January.

7. The winter is more pleasant in this city than the summer; for the rains keep the streets from being as dusty as in the summer, and the chilly morning wind does not blow every day during this season. The lawns are green about many houses, and the trees of heliotrope and fuchsias in the gardens hang full of blossoms.

8. The Mission, as the oldest part of the city is called, is much warmer than the part of the city in front of the hills which shelter these streets from the winds. You find here an old

adobe church, built by Spanish missionaries long
before California became part of our country.

9. San Francisco was only a little village when
gold was first discovered in the Sierras, but now
it is one of the largest cities in the United States.
Tea and silk are imported from Japan and China,
and enormous quantities of wheat, flour, wool,
wines, and fruits are now sent from here to foreign
countries in ships, and to the eastern states by
the railroads which cross the continent. Millions
of dollars are coined here in the mint every year.

10. There are many Chinese in San Francisco,
and a part of the city called Chinatown is inhab-
ited exclusively by them. Many of them are mer-
chants and laundry-men, and others are employed
as servants in the houses and as laborers on the
fruit ranches of the surrounding country.

11. You must go for a drive through Golden
Gate Park. You see people of almost as many
languages as you saw in New Orleans. Fine carriages roll by. In midwinter the grass is green and
the flowers are in bloom. Beyond the park the
drive leads on to the seashore, past sand-hills
not yet planted with trees and grass. You see

a beautiful beach with the waves of the ocean rolling in.

12. The drive goes up a high cliff. Out at sea a little way are hundreds of seals on a group of rocks. Away to the right are the heights on either side of the Golden Gate, and the sails of the vessels on the bay.

13. On the way back to the city, we stop in the park before a monument which was made by Mr. W. W. Story, a famous American sculptor who lives in Rome, and which was given to the city by a rich and generous man. The monument is in honor of Mr. Francis S. Key, the author of the inspiring song beginning —

> "The star-spangled banner,
> Oh! long may it wave
> O'er the land of the free
> And the home of the brave."